FS √ JN

HJ

The Enchanted Voyage

*Also by W. E. D. Ross
in Large Print:*

The Ghost of Oaklands

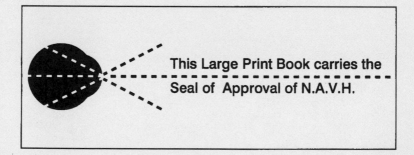

**This Large Print Book carries the
Seal of Approval of N.A.V.H.**

The Enchanted Voyage

W. E. D. Ross

Thorndike Press • Waterville, Maine

Published in 2004 by arrangement with
Maureen Moran Agency.

Thorndike Press® Large Print Candlelight.

The tree indicium is a trademark of Thorndike Press.

The text of this Large Print edition is unabridged.
Other aspects of the book may vary from the original edition.

Set in 16 pt. Plantin by Minnie B. Raven.

Printed in the United States on permanent paper.

Library of Congress Cataloging-in-Publication Data

Ross, W. E. D. (William Edward Daniel), 1912–
    The enchanted voyage / by W.E.D. Ross.
      p. cm.
    ISBN 0-7862-6529-9 (lg. print : hc : alk. paper)
    1. Motion picture industry — Fiction.   2. Ocean liners
— Fiction.   3. Large type books.   I. Title.
PR9199.3.R5996E53 2004
  813′.54—dc22   2004045959

To Walter Pidgeon
Great gentleman of stage and screen

As the Founder/CEO of NAVH, the only national health agency solely devoted to those who, although not totally blind, have an eye disease which could lead to serious visual impairment, I am pleased to recognize Thorndike Press* as one of the leading publishers in the large print field.

Founded in 1954 in San Francisco to prepare large print textbooks for partially seeing children, NAVH became the pioneer and standard setting agency in the preparation of large type.

Today, those publishers who meet our standards carry the prestigious "Seal of Approval" indicating high quality large print. We are delighted that Thorndike Press is one of the publishers whose titles meet these standards. We are also pleased to recognize the significant contribution Thorndike Press is making in this important and growing field.

Lorraine H. Marchi, L.H.D.
Founder/CEO
NAVH

* Thorndike Press encompasses the following imprints: Thorndike, Wheeler, Walker and Large Pr int Press.

Chapter One

"There she is!" Chad Melville, her agent said. "That's the *Britannia*!"

Gale Bond leaned forward to peer out of the taxi window. Her first fleeting glimpse of the majestic old ocean liner was surely a depressing one. It had been raining all day as only it can in New York in May and the Forty-Fourth Street docks, with their grimy sheds and bleak surroundings, looked even more forbidding than usual. For just a moment they passed close to the *Britannia* and the once famed ocean queen towered above them majestically.

Gale couldn't help being impressed even though the fine old ship already showed signs of age and decay. In her brief look at the great liner with its old-fashioned three funnels she realised how antiquated she was. Although in her day she had been as famous as the sleek new *France* or the *United States* she had recently been relegated to bargain-basement West Indies cruises and hadn't made any money on them. So she was due to be scrapped. That probably accounted for the obvious signs of rust on her black hull and the greyish tint of the white-painted upper decks.

But Gale's single glance as the taxi passed on its way to the embarkation sheds had let her see the smoke pouring from its funnels as evidence the old vessel was ready to begin its final voyage. And she was to be part of it. The next several weeks of her life would be spent on the doomed ship. She sat back to stare out at the driving rain again with a thoughtful expression on her pretty face. Was it the rain and the gloomy old docks that made her so apprehensive? Or was it because of the circumstances that had led to her being one of the passengers on this last voyage of a once proud ship? Perhaps it was a combination of both plus her natural fear of the sea.

A fear that had come to her in an understandable way. From girlhood she had heard the story of her aunt's mysterious death repeated. And every so often the papers still revived the eerie circumstances of the famous screen star's last night alive. No one would be ever sure of the facts. Hedda Grant had simply walked out of a gay last-night-at-sea party being held in the *Britannia*'s main ballroom to vanish.

She was never seen alive again. That had been thirty years ago but Hedda Grant had been so well known as a star and the manner of her death so dramatic the story had lived on.

Chad Melville's jowelled, lined face showed mild concern as he stared at her. "You don't seem overjoyed by it all," was his comment. He was one of the senior talent agents in the film field and divided his time between Hollywood and New York. It was he who had brought Gale east.

She managed a faint smile for him, knowing how much effort he had made to get her this job. "I'm sorry," she said. "I suppose it is the weather that is depressing me. These docks look so forbidding in the rain! And the *Britannia* does seem rather dejected."

Chad Melville laughed as the taxi veered towards the shed entrance. "You can't expect them to spend a lot of money sprucing her up. As soon as this voyage is over she goes to the scrapyard." He paused. "I hope you're not allowing those publicity ghost stories to bother you. They were part of getting you the lead in this picture."

"I know," she said with a sigh. She was twenty-three, blonde and pretty in a healthy, direct way. Her face had high

9

cheek bones and her wide blue eyes were amazingly expressive. And although her features lacked the sensitivity of her deceased actress mother who had never risen beyond supporting roles in minor films and she had none of the flamboyant beauty of her famous aunt, Hedda Grant, she had what was known as a good camera face. It and a genuine dramatic talent had kept her well supplied with *ingénue* parts in dozens of filmed television plays. And she had earned small roles in several important movies. But not until Mervin Hawley, the noted producer-director, had decided to lease the doomed *Britannia* to make one of his famous mystery films, had she been offered a starring role in a major film. And she knew that Chad Melville had managed to get her the role by linking the past and the present.

It had been Chad who, on hearing Mervin Hawley had leased the soon to be scrapped *Britannia* from its owners to use as the setting for a new film, had approached the famous director with an idea for a publicity tie-in that would boost the box-office of the picture. He let it be known that Gale, a promising young actress, was available for the starring role and reminded Hawley that she was the niece of the famed star, Hedda Grant, who had vanished aboard the *Britannia* three decades previously. Because Hawley had directed Hedda Grant in many of her films and actually been aboard the liner at the time of her drowning he had at once been interested in the possibilities of the idea.

As a result Gale found herself being tested for the role. The tests proved satisfactory and she had signed contracts for the film. Then a barrage of publicity had been released that made her wish she hadn't. Feature stories were written about Hedda Grant and her picture was run in many publications along with an account of her career and how she had vanished. The general conjecture was that she'd committed suicide by throwing herself overboard in the face of increasing alcoholism and a waning career.

Gale had always had an eerie feeling about the sea, probably due to having heard the story of her aunt's death so often. And for a while she had been on the point of asking to be released from the contract. But Chad had made it clear it could be the beginning of a real career for her. So with feelings of doubt she had come east to sail on the ancient liner and begin making the film. She understood it would take about a month. The only passengers on board would be the cast and crew of the film so just a minimum of space would be occupied on the thirty-five thousand ton vessel.

The taxi came to a halt by the embarkation shed bringing her daydreaming to an end. Chad got out and paid the fare and at once enlisted a blue-smocked porter to look after taking her bags aboard. Her other luggage had gone ahead, including a trunk with many of her costumes for the film which was to be set in a period just before the Second World War. Gale thought the plot of the screenplay followed very closely to the pattern of her famous aunt's life. Perhaps too closely!

Chad helped her out of the taxi and she dodged through the rain and inside the shed with its great high ceilings. It was full of confusion on this dark, dismal day. Baggage porters wheeling carts shouted warnings to clear the way, customs and immigration men worked at their stations, travellers and those seeing them off were grouped about in various spots. Chad led her to an exit not more than half-way down the shed.

"This is the exit we take for the *Britannia*," he said. He was holding her arm

12

and she leaned close to him. As they reached the gangway leading aboard she noticed the group of teenagers clustered at the bottom of it, notebooks and pencils in hand for autographs. Luckily there weren't many and this would likely be because of the weather. As soon as they approached, the youngsters set up a clamour and pushed their books in front of her. She smiled as graciously as she could, signed the minimum possible and let Chad and the uniformed ship's officer on duty there get her away from them and safely *en route* up the gangway.

It was steep and she shivered a little knowing that she was saying goodbye to land for some time. In the days and nights ahead this ghostly old vessel would be her home. Chad was close beside her again and she knew he was being especially solicitous because he was aware of her uneasy state of mind.

"Hawley decided you wouldn't have to go to the press party they're having in the main ballroom," Chad told her as they set foot on a lower deck. "That way you're relieved of the strain and Jane Fair and Steve Benson can take the spotlight. That should make them both happy. Especially Jane."

She gave the agent a small smile as he

led her to a stairway leading to an upper deck. "I know what you mean," she agreed. And she did. Jane Fair and Steve Benson were veteran stars hired for the other principal roles in the film and they were not happy that a newcomer was being given billing above them. Jane Fair had barely spoken to Gale in the few times they had met since the contracts were signed. The thirtyish brunette star had let it be plainly known she resented Gale.

They reached the purser's station and Chad made inquiries about where her cabin was located. It turned out to be on A Deck and a trimly uniformed steward of advanced years was allocated to them to show the way. They followed a long corridor and then mounted a final short flight of broad stairs. This brought them to a wider corridor and it was off this that A20, Gale's suite was located. It consisted of an ample living-room, a large-sized bedroom with real beds and a tiled bath. Chad tipped the steward and looked around admiringly.

"Look at the luxury of the drapes and furniture in these rooms," he said with awe in his voice. "They don't fit ships like this any more." He gave her a knowing glance. "Do you realise this is the same suite occupied by your aunt on the voyage from which she vanished?"

They were standing in the living-room near her luggage. She gave him a despairing little glance and flopping into a nearby chair took the rainproof kerchief from her shining blonde hair. "Don't remind me," she said.

Chad took out a cigar and bit off its end. "I'd like to leave you in a better mood," he said. "You should be happy about this."

"I am," she said with a wan smile. "I'm also a little awed and frightened."

"You've got nothing to worry about," Chad assured her as he lit the cigar and took a puff. "I saw those tests. You're going to be great."

"I just wish we were making the film in Hollywood or anywhere on land," she said.

He smiled. "If they'd done that you wouldn't be the star. Count yourself lucky."

"I'll try."

"Being aboard this ship for its last cruise should be an experience in itself," her agent went on. "And they say the sea is as calm as glass off Cape Cod at this time of year. They're going to circle out there until the filming is all done. So you don't need to worry."

15

At that moment the air was rent with a doleful blast from the funnel of the old liner. A warning that it would not be long before she sailed. Gale stood up nervously and went forward to say goodbye to the agent.

He kissed her in a fatherly manner and with a concerned expression on his heavy face told her, "I want you to give the performance of your life. Forget about everything else and just do a great acting job!"

"I'll try," she promised.

"I'll stop by and speak to Hawley in the ballroom on my way ashore," the agent told her. "Don't worry about anything." And then he left her.

As soon as the cabin door closed after him she began to have feelings of fear once more. She glanced around the ornate room with its crystal chandelier, rich panelling and thick carpets. It spoke of the elegance of a bygone era. It fairly cried of yesterday. And then a frown crossed her pretty face as she went across to the exquisitely carved walnut dresser with its large mirror and picked up the big framed photograph on it. It was her late aunt, Hedda Grant, in one of her familiar poses. Her aunt had been blonde like herself and this was about the only similarity between them. It struck her that in contrast to her mother, who had been Hedda's younger sister, the star had a very cold, hard face. And in spite of the smile she wore in the photograph Gale had the sensation the woman who had vanished from this suite thirty years before was glaring at her.

She set the photograph down and turned around and at once gave a gasp of surprise. There was someone else in the room with her. Someone who had entered so quietly she hadn't heard them. Now the newcomer nodded and spoke to her.

"I see you are admiring your aunt's photograph," he said. He was a stranger to Gale. A rather small, frail man with iron-grey hair, and a pinched, wrinkled face. He wore heavy-lensed horn-rimmed glasses that enlarged his eyes to give them an owl-like staring look and he had a high-pitched, squeaky voice.

"You startled me," Gale said.

"I didn't intend to," the small man said. "You seemed wrapped up in the photo when I came in. I didn't like to disturb you. I'd like to introduce myself, my name is Francois Mailet, I'm the make-up artist for the film. I'll be taking care of you."

Gale went over and shook hands with him. "I'm glad to know you," she said. She

17

was still somewhat startled by the unexpected appearance of the thin old man and decided he couldn't have knocked hard on the door or she would have heard him. His hand was damp and clammy and she was glad to let it go.

The owlish eyes studied her. "I have looked after the make-up for all Mr. Hawley's recent pictures," the man said. "Jane Fair won't let anyone else near her."

She smiled. "I'm glad to know I'm going to be in such good hands."

Francois Mailet continued to stare at her. "You have a good face. You'll photograph well."

"I always have," she said, a little resentful of the eccentric's intrusion and comments.

The make-up man's pinched face showed no reaction to this. He went on with, "But you are not the beauty Hedda Grant was. Nor do I think you are likely to have her talent."

Gale frowned. "You knew her?"

The little man nodded. "She was a genius."

"My mother was an actress too," Gale reminded him.

Francois Mailet showed scorn. "I saw her work often. Run of the mill. Nothing

18

more. At least you have a big chance thanks to the publicity story about your aunt's death."

"I had to pass a test as well before they gave me the job," Gale said pointedly, startled at the make-up man's brazenness.

Francois Mailet seemed to sense he had gone too far. "I mean no offence," he said quickly in his high-pitched voice. "I merely wanted to offer my good wishes and introduce myself." He paused. "This is a fine old ship. What a pity it is to be her last voyage."

"Still it is dated," Gale said.

The make-up man's pinched face held a look of scorn and the eyes behind the thick glasses showed anger. "That's what is wrong with this country. We have no respect for the old. Youth is worshipped. It has cost us far too much!"

Gale was surprised by this outburst. "I suppose there is truth in what you say."

The thin old man shrugged. "No one listens. No one cares! I'll see you on the set, Miss Bond." And with a bob of his head he went out.

She stared after him with a frown. The whole interview had been as incredible as it was unexpected. She was almost certain the old man had deliberately walked into the room without giving any warning, had intruded on her privacy by intention. She could see that he would be difficult to work with and probably because of his long association with Hollywood had known everyone of her aunt's era. But he must be competent or Mervin Hawley wouldn't give him steady employment. There could be sentiment involved in this as well since Hawley was now definitely one of the oldest of the active directors.

Was this a sample of what she might expect? Would she be continually compared to the famous Hedda Grant and found wanting? Before she had not had this problem. The acceptance she had won in Hollywood had been strictly on her own talents. She had never used the name of her famous relative when seeking jobs. Her accomplishments might have been modest but she had won them by herself. Now the spotlight had been turned on the fact she was Hedda Grant's niece, starring in a film that was loosely like the story of the famed star's life. Every bit of publicity had been focused on Hedda Grant and the macabre way in which she had met her death. Again Gale felt uneasy about the project and uncomfortable aboard the doomed ship. Who had put the photograph of her aunt on her dresser? The publicity department no doubt. It was likely their grisly touch to catch the eye of the Press whom they had earlier shown through the old vessel.

She felt a certain desire to get away from the cabin. To seek someone to talk with. Anything but to stay here in this musty, haunted atmosphere of another day alone. This garish suite with its memories of her long dead aunt. Perhaps it was ridiculous of her to feel as she did. In the three decades since Hedda Grant's death a multitude of people must have occupied this suite. But for Gale there was only one person associated with it. She gave the smiling hard face of the portrait another swift glance then she picked up her rain kerchief and left the cabin quickly.

She was just outside in the corridor when the *Britannia* blew new warning blasts that fairly vibrated the whole ship. And then there was the sound of voices from the other end of the corridor. This would be some of the party group leaving now that the ship was about to sail. She hurried along the dark corridor in the opposite direction and went out onto the forward deck. It was still raining hard and she tied the protecting kerchief in place and tightened her raincoat around her as she

21

gazed at the docks and the shrouded towers of Manhattan in the far background. It was an imposing spectacle at any time but a somewhat gloomy one on this late rainy afternoon.

A flight of steps led up to an observation deck and on impulse she decided to go up there and watch as the old vessel cast off from the docks and backed out into the greasy, polluted waters of the Hudson at this mid-Manhattan point before heading out past the Statue of Liberty, Staten Island and toward the Atlantic.

Leaning against the railing she stared down at the docks so far below and steeled herself as another great blast came from the ship's horn. The last of the visitors had made their way to the dock and the gangways had been hauled in. Now the tugs had appeared to guide the big ship out and the men on the docks with the lines stared up at her with grave expressions. She could see there was a sadness in their faces at the knowledge this was to be the last voyage of one of the true ocean monarchs. A small group had gathered at the rails on the lower deck and she spotted the tall producer-director, Mervin Hawley, among them. He was leaning over the rail waving and calling out to some crony on the docks far below, wearing no hat or coat in the pouring rain, a handsome, distinguished figure of a man with a head of white hair that indicated his sixty-odd years. He had once been an actor and still carried himself erect and handled his body with style. Grouped around him were other members of the cast and production crew.

"Quite a moment, isn't it?" this was said to her by a pleasant male voice.

She turned to see a tall, striking young man with reddish hair and a trim moustache of the same shade had taken a place at the rail beside her. He was hatless but had on a light raincoat. His serious, intellectual-looking face wore a smile.

"I find it so," she admitted.

"I wanted to get away from the crowd so I could take it all in properly," he said. "I'm a writer. It's part of my stock in trade to store up odd moments like this."

It was her turn to smile. "I can understand." And then, "Don't let me divert you. I mean, don't feel you have to make conversation."

He laughed lightly. "Don't misunderstand me. I rather enjoy sharing this with someone. It's just the crowd that would be fatal. Too much confusion to record impressions."

The old vessel gave another great blast and they didn't try to speak for a moment. Then she began to move away from the dock. She glanced at the Manhattan towers slipping away and felt again the sense of uneasiness she had known from first sighting the *Britannia.*

The young man turned to her with a smile as the blast ended. "The old girl's still in good voice."

"Those blasts terrify me," she admitted. "I'm not fond of the sea or great ships like this. I feel like the poem that goes, 'There are certain things, as a spider, a ghost . . . That I hate, but the thing that I hate the most, Is a thing they call the Sea'."

"You know who wrote that, of course?" he asked.

She shook her head. "I'm not sure that I do."

"Lewis Carroll, the *Alice In Wonderland* author," he said. "And so you echo his sentiments about the sea?"

"I'm afraid so." The great liner was swinging around now and every plate in her seemed to be creaking with the motion. Shortly the tugs would cast off and she would head alone out toward the Atlantic over which she had reigned for so long.

The young man eyed her sharply. "Or is

it just this ship that frightens you because of the fact your aunt met her death aboard it?"

She gave him a surprised glance. "You know me then?"

"We aren't a very large complement aboard this time," he said genially. "May I introduce myself, Miss Bond. I'm Jack Henderson. I've written the screenplay for the film. I'm aboard for last minute revisions to fit the surroundings."

"I'm glad to know you," she said. "From what I've read of the script you know all about my aunt's life." There was a reproving twinkle in her large blue eyes.

"It isn't actually a carbon copy of the real events," he protested. "I have included a mystery angle and picked a character as your aunt's murderer and the one who killed her and threw her overboard."

"That is a deviation from the facts," she said thoughtfully. "From all the accounts I've read the conclusion seems to be she committed suicide. The leap into the ocean was her own decision."

"I know," Jack Henderson nodded. "But then it will always be a mystery. What really happened has never been truly documented. Her husband died soon after in a plane wreck. There are not many people

25

still living who were on the ship that night or who even knew her intimately."

"I only know what my mother told me about her," Gale admitted. "They weren't very close as some sisters are."

"So I gathered," he said quietly. And by way of explanation, "Before I wrote the screenplay I spent a lot of time delving into Hedda Grant's background. I also talked to all the people I could concerning her life and mysterious death. I think I can call myself an authority on your aunt."

"I'd begun to forget about her and what had happened," Gale admitted. "Then Mervin Hawley decided to make this film on the *Britannia* and my agent thought we had a special angle to offer him."

"You had. He was lucky to get you as the star." He paused. "You're not afraid of the ship being bad luck for you?"

The question hit her in such a tender spot she stared at him in wonder. "Why do you ask that?"

"I can see that it might," Jack Henderson said, frowning a little. "You know there is a rumour that your aunt's ghost still haunts the *Britannia*?"

She stared at him. "No. I hadn't ever heard it stated as a fact although I'm not surprised there have been such rumours."

"I came across the story when I was doing my research," he went on. "You'd be surprised the number of people who have sworn they've seen her walking alone on these decks. And the odd thing is that people who wouldn't have any way of knowing have been able to describe the clothes she wore on that last night."

Gale gave a small gasp. "That sounds incredible! It must have been a coincidence or perhaps they read about it somewhere."

"I considered that," he agreed. "But these reports came in over the space of several years from a number of different people strangers to each other. And as far as I know none of them read the original accounts of your aunt's disappearance."

There was a pause. Then she said, "How do you account for it?"

He stared down at the grey water of the Hudson. "I'm not completely a cynic. I believe there is such a thing as thought transference. Perhaps it extends to the spirit world. The impression of Hedda Grant is so strong on this ship that it may convey itself to travellers on it years after her death."

Gale gave a small shiver and turned to watch the rapidly approaching Statue of Liberty. "I don't admit to a belief in ghosts," she said.

"A lot of people who don't admit to a belief in them still hesitate to enter dark old houses," Jack Henderson said in a teasing voice.

She looked at him directly. "Are you deliberately trying to frighten me?"

"Not at all," he assured her. "But I did want to tell you what I'd found out before it reached you twisted out of all proportion by some publicity men."

Gale sighed. "I think they've made too much of the mystery. She was an unhappy woman and she killed herself. Why not let her rest?"

"Whenever there is a hint of mystery in the death of a celebrity the story never rests. It gets retold down through the years. I wonder how many of Hedda Grant's contemporaries could command the amount of newspaper space today that she does? Her suicide brought her a kind of notorious immortality."

"I suppose I'm to blame in a way," she said, staring off across the foggy water. "I shouldn't have agreed to the publicity."

"Surely you're not afraid the ghost of a jealous Hedda will try revenge?"

She arched an eyebrow. "If I'm to believe you it might happen."

The young man drew a copy of the late

afternoon paper from his pocket and opened it to the photos of herself and Hedda side by side with an account of the *Britannia*'s sailing and the making of the film. He turned the paper over and pointing to a small item headed, "Madman At Large", he said, "The amusing thing is your publicity people and the Press missed the chance for extra headlines. Two days ago Joseph Holland escaped from an upstate mental hospital. He's still free as the paper notes. But what they don't say is that he was once a prominent Hollywood artist and not only did a famous portrait of your aunt but had a love affair with her." He paused significantly. "And for the real clincher he was a passenger on this ship the night Hedda vanished. They missed a real story in that!"

"I wonder if he remembers," Gale said thoughtfully. "If he knows about the *Britannia* and what is to happen to her. Could he help clear the mystery of Hedda?"

Chapter Two

The young man in the trench coat gazed at her with mild surprise. "I hardly think so," he said. "Holland was coming back from France with his wife on the voyage from which your aunt disappeared. I have never heard their names linked as seeing a lot of each other. In fact I believe there had been a quarrel between them."

"Oh?" The *Britannia* had now cast off the tugs and was ploughing through the rougher waters of the harbour on its way to the ocean. The rain had let up a little but the great ship was wreathed in a misty greyness that cut down vision to a minimum and it was cooler now the liner was gathering speed.

"Something about her not approving of the portrait Holland had done of her," the writer went on. "From my questioning I received the impression they weren't even speaking by the time the voyage began."

Gale smiled ruefully. "Perhaps they had an argument and he pitched her over the side. That is, if his lunatic tendencies were showing up even then."

"He didn't have his breakdown until about ten years ago," Jack Henderson said. "I believe it was mainly the result of too much drinking and a generally failing health."

"And he's been in a sanatorium ever since?"

"Off and on. He's done some work at various times. Very strange work in contrast to his former paintings. Most of the new ones are distorted and the figures pale, willowy things like ghosts floating in pale green liquid."

Gale raised her eyebrow. "Doesn't that strengthen my theory he may have been Hedda Grant's murderer? Perhaps it has played on his conscience all these years and he thinks of her body floating in the ocean. That is why he paints these odd figures."

The young man laughed. "You make an excellent point if a somewhat macabre one. And you could be right. Wilder things have been proven true. I don't know whether he had access to newspapers and read about the film and you. At any rate he's escaped."

She glanced up at the young man with the serious face and the small red moustache. She was leaning against the rail of the upper deck with her back toward the water. "And he is still at large?"

"He was when this edition of the paper came out about three hours ago."

Her pretty face showed concern. "If he read about the film and the *Britannia* being used he might have headed straight here."

"I rather doubt that," he said with a headshake. "The place he escaped from is pretty far upstate. I can't imagine his reaching the city without being caught somewhere along the way."

Her eyes searched his face. "But if he did?"

"Then I can scarcely see his getting on board. You must have noted there was a ship's officer at every gangway. Hawley gave strict orders to see that only those with proper credentials were allowed aboard. He wanted to guard against curiosity seekers and unauthorised newspaper and magazine people."

"And so you think there is no danger of a mad Joseph Holland having secreted himself somewhere aboard?"

"I'd consider it a minimum risk," the young man assured her. "And aren't you satisfied to be plagued merely with the ghost of your late aunt? I should think that would provide enough unpleasantness for the trip."

"More than satisfied," she said with a sigh. "I know it's all a lot of nonsense talked up to create interest in the film. But it still bothers me a little. I suppose because her death was never explained and because of my natural fear of the sea."

"I understand," he said sympathetically. "You look cold?"

"It is chilly now," she admitted. "I didn't mind the rain at the docks it was so warm. But there is quite a breeze out here in the harbour."

"It is liable to be even colder as night falls," the young man said. "I suggest we go down to the forward lounge. I doubt if it has been discovered by the company yet. It should make an excellent place to sit for a while, warm up and enjoy a little refreshment."

"It sounds like an excellent idea," Gale agreed with a final glance out over the water. "It's so foggy there is nothing to see here."

They made their way down to A Deck and Jack Henderson led her to the door leading to the forward lounge. They met no one along the way. All of the party with producer Mervin Hawley had left the railing as soon as the ship pulled away from the dock. In a ship as large as this one the comparatively small crew and cast of the film production would take very little space. Gale felt they would be lost in the vastness of the great vessel.

And the situation in the lounge bore out her conviction. A single bartender stood idly behind the circular bar with its splendid array of bottles suitably spotlighted. The almost dark lounge was empty except for him. There was no one seated at the tables or the bar stools.

"My prediction was pretty good," Jack told her.

They decided to sit at a table that was suitably remote from the bar. The white-coated man came and took their order. Then they began to talk across the table.

"This is your first really big break, isn't it?" Jack Henderson said.

She nodded. "Yes. I suppose you could say I owe it to my aunt."

He smiled. "Do you think she would enjoy your getting it?"

"I'm not sure," she said frankly. "I wouldn't be too certain. She was always jealous of my mother and never did anything to help her get parts. In fact, my

34

mother was never in a Hedda Grant picture. She made her biggest success after Hedda's death."

"I would imagine that gave your mother great satisfaction."

"I'm sure it did."

The waiter returned with their order. When he had gone again Jack Henderson said, "I talked to a lot of people who knew Hedda. Their opinion seemed to be that she was, at her best, a good actress but off screen they regarded her as a pretty awful person." He looked apologetic. "No offence intended I assure you."

She smiled demurely over her glass of wine. "None taken, I assure you. I know all about her reputation. From an authority, my mother."

"Then it all was true?"

"I'm afraid so."

He sat back with a sigh. "Yet, none of that came over on the screen. She was beloved by millions. And that is proven by the fact she is still news today. And thirty years have gone by since that night she vanished from this ship."

Gale said, "She wasn't doing so well at the time, was she?"

"No. She'd been finding it hard to get jobs in Hollywood and had taken an offer to do a film in London." His expression was revealing. "And that was in the days when London films weren't the quality product they are now."

"Her career was really on the wane."

"That's about it. Her husband, Jerry Hall, was also her agent. He was on the voyage back with her along with a maid who'd been with her for several years. I'd liked to have talked with Jerry Hall but that wasn't possible, you'll remember he was killed in a plane accident about six months after your aunt vanished."

Gale nodded. "Yes. My mother was terribly shocked that it should happen so soon after Hedda's death. It seemed as if fate had marked them out."

"I tried to trace the maid," the young man went on. "I felt she could tell me a lot. But she seemed to have vanished almost as thoroughly as your aunt after the ship docked. Apparently instead of returning to Hollywood she took another job in the New York area. No one in Hollywood ever heard of her again."

She frowned slightly. "That's odd. Was she an older woman?"

"From all accounts she wasn't old at all. As young as your aunt and perhaps younger. She had very little social life so I wasn't able to contact many people who knew her even casually."

Gale eyed him with amused interest. "You've become terribly involved with it all, haven't you?"

"I'm afraid that's right," he admitted, glancing down at his drink with some confusion. "When Mervin Hawley assigned me to do the screenplay I'd hardly more than heard Hedda Grant mentioned as one of the old-time greats."

"But her magic was still strong enough to trap you," Gale said with a smile. "In spite of her private reputation of being hateful I understand she could be a true enchantress when she made up her mind."

"A long line of male conquests prove that."

She teased him. "And you're the last of them?"

His serious face showed a faint smile. "I wouldn't say that. I haven't been caught up in any fancy legend. But tracking down her story has become an obsession with me. Even now that I've finished the screenplay for Hawley. I still think there are mysteries to be solved, apart from her death, and that some of the people on board this ship could solve them."

"Oh? Who, for instance?"

"Mervin Hawley for one. He and Hedda were good friends for a long time. He was one of those hosting the party she attended before vanishing. I don't think he's ever forgotten that night. And that was why he decided to make this picture. To try and get it down and settle it in his own mind."

"But your story is pure fiction, isn't it?"

Jack Henderson nodded. "Yes. My angle of her romance with the ship's Chief Officer and his being the one who murdered her is purely imaginary. But I do think she had a lover on board who turned on her because of jealousy and brought about her death."

"Now we're back to the mad artist, Joseph Holland," she said.

"He wasn't mad then and I wasn't thinking of him especially," the man across the table from her said. "I'm sure it was someone else. But I haven't decided who."

She took another sip of her wine. "Perhaps you'll find out before the *Britannia* heads back to land."

"I'm going to try," he said seriously.

As he finished speaking the door to the lounge opened and a tall, handsome man with a classic profile and hard, blue eyes entered and went straight to the bar. He wore a dark sports coat and grey trousers and had a fancy red and green cravat tied loosely under the weary, handsome face. He ordered a drink and when it was served downed half of it quickly.

Jack smiled. "Well, at least someone has discovered our retreat."

"An important someone," she said. And naming the leading man, she asked, "Do you know Steve Benson?"

"We're acquaintances," Jack said. "I wouldn't call us friends. He's not the easiest man in Hollywood to get along with."

Gale looked woeful. "He's been wonderful with me compared to Jane Fair. When we posed for the publicity pictures she didn't even speak to me."

"Don't let it bother you," Jack said. "It's just she knows you're younger and prettier and bound to steal the picture from her."

The handsome actor's eyes had by now become accustomed to the gloom of the room and spotting them at their table Steven Benson picked up his drink from the bar and came over to them.

"Mind if I intrude?" he asked pleasantly. And without waiting for a reply he pulled a chair from an adjoining table and sat down with them. His classic features wore a melancholy look. "Was there ever a more forlorn project than this?" he wanted to know.

Gale smiled. "I'm not sure I follow you."

"My dear girl," Steve Benson protested dramatically. "This is complete idiocy on Mervin Hawley's part. He could just as well have filmed this dubious feature in the comfort and privacy of the home lot in Hollywood. Instead he has us dragged across the continent to suffer needlessly on this ghost ship."

Jack Henderson said, "But think of all the publicity it has gotten the film even before it is made. I'd call that a stroke of genius on Hawley's part."

The actor's cold blue eyes regarded the young writer with disdain. "I still say he's mad. Can you imagine what it has cost him to charter this old tub? And I'm not even certain she is seaworthy any longer. If we're not lucky we might all end up at the bottom of the Atlantic along with the fabulous Hedda!"

"I hardly think that," Gale said. "The *Britannia* has been in service right along. And I'm sure the authorities wouldn't allow her to sail if she wasn't in proper condition."

Steve Benson regarded her haughtily. "I'm not so easily convinced," he said in a stern voice. "I have known such things happen. And Hawley has a way of swaying people when he wants something."

Risking the actor's wrath, Jack Henderson asked, "Why did you take on a role in the film if you feel this way?"

For a moment Steve Benson looked startled then he quickly covered up by saying, "I owe Hawley a favour and he seems to think I'm indispensable to the success of the venture."

Jack smiled. "Then you do think it will be a success?"

Steve Benson frowned. "I think there may be some surprises come out of all this. I have the feeling Hawley was wrong to probe into the past and drag Hedda's story out on the front pages again. There was tragedy before and I think the *Britannia* could well see tragedy again."

"You interest me," Jack said. "Why do you say that?"

The actor was silent a moment, his handsome face dimly visible in the shadowed lounge. Then with great drama he announced, "Because I know people who have seen Hedda's ghost aboard this ship."

Jack gave Gale a meaningful glance. And she turned to the actor. "But all those stories are pure fantasy!"

The classic profile went stern. "I'm

sorry," he said in his sonorous voice. "I don't agree."

Jack Henderson spoke up. "Then you surely must have some basis for your opinion?"

"I do," Steve Benson nodded slowly.

"Who told you this story?" Gale wanted to know.

He turned a bleak blue eye on her. "No one had to tell me," he said. "I used this vessel myself some years ago when she was still in trans-Atlantic service. And I saw Hedda Grant's ghost with my own eyes!"

It was a startling statement and delivered with such conviction that it brought silence to the three gathered at the small table in the shadowed lounge. The veteran ship swayed just a little and there was the groaning, creaking sound of ancient metal plates again as if in protest to what had been said. As if the *Britannia* resented this intrusion on her secrets.

At last, Gale said, "You sound very sure."

His eyes met hers. "It is not often I find myself seeing a ghost, Miss Bond. I am, indeed, very sure. I had known Hedda slightly before she vanished. I was a boy in those days just beginning in the business. So I knew her well by sight. It was ten years later that I was returning from England on this ship. By a peculiar coincidence the last night out, I was walking alone on A Deck when I saw a figure come out of the darkness toward me. As she came nearer I saw it was a woman and could make out the details of her dress. She was wearing an out-dated hat of a decade before, a small pillbox affair with a long flowing veil that reached to her chin line. She had on some sort of dark suit whose length was ridiculously out of style. But it was the hat and veil that caught my attention. Hedda had always worn this type of hat and veil. She had been wearing just such an outfit the night she vanished I was to learn later. But on the foggy night I've described I did not know that. And as she came close to me I could clearly make out her features. I called her name. As much in fright as anything else. There was no one else in sight at the time and just the booming of the ship's foghorn and the rush of the waves against her hull to break the shrouded silence." The actor paused.

Jack said, "Did she answer you?"

Steve Benson shook his head. "No. I called her name a second time since I was so certain it was Hedda and I had some wild idea that she had been in hiding in

Europe somewhere and booked passage on this ship again. That she was returning to life and her friends. But she seemed neither to see me nor hear me. She kept on walking straight along that fog-ridden deck, her eyes vacant and staring at some distant point. I watched as she vanished in the mist, chilled by fear and beginning to believe for the first time that this was no living Hedda but a phantom."

"And then what?" Gale asked tensely, the actor's recital in the gloomy lounge building her own fears.

He frowned. "I did a stupid thing. I made up my mind to follow her. I turned and hurried along in the fog in the direction in which she'd gone and after a moment I caught a glimpse of her ahead. I shouted again but she did not turn. Then after a moment she went inside. I noted where she'd gone and followed. I caught a glimpse of her in the soft light of the corridor as she unlocked the door of her cabin. She had gone inside when I reached it and I knocked on the door. Of course she didn't answer. I knocked again and I waited."

Jack Henderson was also plainly caught up by the actor's story. He said, "What happened next?"

Steve Benson stared down at his empty glass with an odd expression. "I was still there in the corridor waiting when a steward came by. I said I wanted to speak with the woman occupying the cabin and he stared at me in surprise. It seemed he thought I must be out of my head. The cabin before which I was waiting had not been booked for that crossing. It was empty!"

Jack frowned. "Did you make sure of this?"

The handsome leading man gave him one of his weary, derisive smiles. "I imagined you might be going to ask me that. Naturally, I told him he was wrong. That I had seen a woman unlock the door and go in that supposedly empty cabin. I raised such a fuss he finally called an officer who opened the door and showed me through the rooms."

"And they were empty?" Gale asked in a hushed voice.

"Of course," the actor said bitterly. "I'd been drinking a little and they both looked at me as if I'd had too much. But there I stood in that empty suite feeling like a fool. I apologised for the trouble I'd caused and got away as quickly as I could. But I hadn't lost my head so badly that I didn't do one thing."

45

"Such as?" Jack asked.

"I was careful to take the number of the cabin. And the following day I checked and found out it was the identical cabin Hedda Grant had occupied at the time of her disappearance. That was all I needed to know. I had seen a ghost."

Gale swallowed hard. "I think I can tell you the number of the cabin," she said quietly.

"Really?" the actor showed mild interest.

"A20, wasn't it?"

He nodded. "Right. How did you know?"

"I happen to be in it now," she said in the same low voice.

Jack Henderson spoke up. "It's the logical thing. I mean as a follow-up to the publicity. Hawley was bound to put you in there since you're playing the role of your aunt."

"Of course," Steve Benson agreed. And he gave her a sympathetic glance. "I don't envy you your quarters, my dear." He paused. "And neither do I envy you your demanding role as Jane Fair most certainly does."

Gale smiled ruefully. "She hasn't bothered to hide that from me."

"It is too bad," Steve Benson said with a

sigh. "After all Hawley has put you through to get this part I must warn you Jane is doing everything she can to take it away from you. She's been giving our producer a very unpleasant time."

Jack Henderson showed surprise. "But I don't see how she can manage that now," he said. "We're at sea with the company selected. It's too late for cast changes. I mean there is no one to take Jane's role even if she wheedled Hawley into allowing her to replace Miss Bond."

"Don't count on that," the actor told him. "Jane has it all figured out. I heard her telling Hawley. There is a minor female role being played by Kate Paxton. You remember her. She used to be a star. It's Jane's idea that she take over for Miss Bond, Kate replace her as the star and Miss Bond be shifted to the minor role."

"But I have a contract!" Gale protested.

Steve Benson sighed. "You'd get your star's pay all right," he admitted. "But if you read the small print in your contract I think Hawley does have the right to demote you in the cast. Or so I gathered by the conversation I heard between them at the party this afternoon."

Gale turned to Jack Henderson in her upset. "Do you really believe that?"

The young writer looked troubled. "It's very likely Jane is raising a row. I know she's been complaining about receiving second billing to you. But I'd say Hawley is just humouring her because he needs her for the part she's cast in now. I wouldn't let it worry me."

Steve Benson was studying her sympathetically. "I may have sounded the alarm a bit too strongly," he admitted. "No doubt our young friend's opinion is a sound one."

"I'll speak to Mr. Hawley tonight," she said. "I have a right to know what he's planning to do."

The leading man looked suddenly disconcerted.

"Don't mention that I told you," he begged. "In fact I think it would be better if you didn't say anything to him at all. Just listen and observe before you bring up a subject which you may not have to bring up at all."

She said, "What do you mean?"

"We'll all be at the Captain's table for dinner," Steve Benson said. "You'll have a chance to talk to Hawley then without making an issue of the matter. There is to be only one sitting for meals since the *Britannia* dining salon is such a large one and we have such a small group. I imagine we'll be lost in the vast old room."

Jack nodded. "I've seen it. All mahogany panelling and great crystal chandeliers. It's like the dining hall of some great old castle."

The leading man frowned. "Could be a fire trap. They're not putting that sort of wood panelling in the modern liners. I tell you I'll feel a lot better when we're back on land. Another crazy idea is taking us out off Cape Cod. That is where the *Andrea Doria* was rammed and sunk!"

"I don't think anything like that is liable to happen again in these days of improved radar," the young writer said.

The leading man stood up with a wise expression on his handsome face. "In this kind of weather anything could happen!" And with a nod for Gale, "Beware of the ghost, Miss Bond."

Jack said, "Are you really so sure you saw a ghost after all? It might have been one of the other passengers." He smiled. "And you admit you were drinking."

Steve Benson shook his head. "Not so much that I'd see someone go into a cabin and vanish in thin air." He leaned forward confidentially. "I'll tell you how else I know it was Hedda Grant's ghost. I found out later she always wore a special kind of

49

perfume, had it made up for her exclusively, a kind of rose with a different overtone of sweetness. When that figure passed me in the fog I could smell that perfume. It trailed after her."

And with a grave nod he turned and left them. As soon as he'd gone out onto the deck Jack Henderson glanced at her. The red-haired young writer had a perplexed expression on his pleasant face.

"I wouldn't let Benson upset you," he said. "I think he was putting on a performance for our benefit."

"I don't know," she sighed. "He was awfully convincing."

"Part of his trade," Jack Henderson reminded her. "And it could be he is on Jane Fair's side even though he's pretending to be your friend. This ghost story could be part of a scheme to frighten you and make you give up as star."

Her eyes opened wide. "Do you think so?"

"It wouldn't surprise me," he said. "I'd take his story with a grain of salt."

Gale was encouraged by the young man's words. After they talked a while longer she began to feel less nervous even though the atmosphere in the lounge was gloomy. Then she realised it was growing late and time for her to start getting dressed for her first dinner on board the *Britannia*.

When they left the lounge it was more foggy than before and almost dark. The rain had become a heavy mist and the great throaty horn of the old vessel gave off with a fog warning at short intervals. Jack saw her to the door of A20. And with a reassuring smile warned her not to lose her courage.

As he walked away she unlocked the cabin and went inside. The light was not on in the living-room of the suite and it was almost dark in there. She was about to reach for the switch when she was suddenly aware of a subtle something enveloping her. It brought her a cold feeling of sheer terror as she realised the room was filled with the odour of rose perfume! A different sort of rose perfume from any she had ever smelled before! At once her mind went back to Steve Benson's story of the ghost!

Hovering between an impulse to turn and run from the room and merely switching on the light she allowed her frightened eyes to quickly scan the room and the bedroom beyond. Her heart skipped a beat as she a saw figure move in the shadowed bedroom.

Chapter Three

Gale was paralysed with terror for a moment. Her eyes strained to see what lurked in the shadows of the other room. She wasn't even able to reach the short distance to the wall light switch but stood mute in the murky living-room wondering what obscene thing loitered there just a few feet away. And now she saw the figure move closer and she could tell that it was a woman. She feared she might faint! All she could think of was that Hedda Grant's spirit must hate her as the star had hated her mother in life. And now she had come to take her revenge for Gale's temerity in planning to enact her role in this film.

Then the phantom spoke. And it was the voice of an old woman. She said, "Is it you, Miss Bond?"

It took seconds before Gale could find her voice and weakly answer. "Yes. I'm Gale Bond."

The elderly woman with the slight Irish lilt in her voice said warmly, "Let me welcome you to the *Britannia*, Miss Bond. I'm

Maggie Dever, your maid."

"I see."

"I hope I didn't frighten you, Miss Bond," the slight figure in the shadows said with apology in her tone. She moved across to the spot where Gale stood and turned on the living-room light. Suddenly she was revealed as a slightly bent white-haired woman with a motherly face. She wore a maid's black outfit with white apron and cap.

"You did give me a start," Gale admitted.

The gentle face of Maggie Dever showed a smile. "It's a bad habit I have of going about in the dark. I know the place so well I could take care of it with my eyes shut. Sometimes I don't bother with the lights at all. At least not until its pitch black."

"I understand," Gale said.

"I have your bed turned down," Maggie Dever told her. "And any help you need all you have to do is ring the bell in your bedroom and I'll be right here."

Gale was gradually recovering her poise. She told the maid, "Thank you. But I think I can manage very well alone."

The veteran Maggie Dever looked unhappy at this. "I'd be more than glad to help you, Miss. I've been looking after the people in this section since the *Britannia* was first built. It seems strange that this is to be the end."

"I suppose it does."

The old woman nodded. "Lucky it is time for me to retire as well. I'm too old to get used to a new ship." She managed a smile for Gale. "So I'd like to be especially useful on this last voyage."

"I'm sure you can help me when we begin the film," Gale assured her.

Maggie Dever brightened. "They tell me it's to be all about Hedda Grant. She was the beauty, I tell you! What a great star she was! I was always her maid when she sailed on the *Britannia*. And she wouldn't cross the Atlantic on another ship. It seemed strange that she should vanish from her in the end."

Gale was interested. She said, "Were you her maid on that last trip?"

"Of course. I always was."

"Did you notice anything strange? Anything that you realised afterward might have given you a hint of what she was going to do?"

The old woman looked uncertain. Then she leaned forward confidentially, "You're her niece aren't you? I hear you're to play poor Miss Hedda in the picture."

"Yes."

Maggie Dever sighed. "Then I guess I can tell you. Things weren't the same that last time. After all the trips I looked after her I was hardly allowed in here at all. She had her own maid with her. Nasty little thing with glasses! I never liked that one! And it's my belief she encouraged Miss Hedda in her drinking."

"She was drinking a lot then?"

The old woman nodded. "A fair shame! And that husband of hers didn't help. He was a sly one. Don't you doubt that! After it happened they wouldn't let me in here either." The old woman shook her head. "I tell you there was something mysterious going on."

Gale stared at the old woman. "In what way?"

"I suppose I'm talking too much for my own good, Miss," the old woman said nervously. "But I saw plenty. Maybe more than poor Miss Hedda did what with her being always under the drink. I came in here once and found her husband with that maid in his arms. Roared at me and ordered me out, he did!"

"You think Jerry Hall was carrying on an affair with her maid?"

The old woman sniffed. "That's the way it looked to me and that's no lie! He came to me afterward and apologised. Very awkward about it. Asked me not to say anything to Miss Hedda. Went on a long-winded bit of nonsense about things not being what they seemed. Said the maid had gotten something in her eye and he'd been trying to help get it out."

"But you didn't believe him."

"You're right, I didn't," the old woman said promptly. "And when Miss Hedda vanished like she did I had an idea he and that maid could tell more about it than anyone else."

She frowned at the old woman. "You really think they might have had a part in my aunt's death?"

Maggie Dever's pale, wrinkled face took on a wary expression. "It's not for the likes of me to say, Miss. In all my thirty years on the *Britannia* I've known how to keep my place."

"Have you ever told this story to anyone else?"

"Not a soul except Baldwin, the steward for A Deck at the time, and he's been dead these fourteen years! Poor dear Baldwin! What a comfort he was! You don't get stewards of his sort these days! How I've missed him! This young lot aboard now don't take any interest in their work. Not like Baldwin!"

Gale sighed. "Perhaps you should have mentioned some of this to the proper authorities at the time."

Maggie Dever shook her head sadly. "It wouldn't have done any good, Miss. I could have talked my head off and they would have denied everything. And who would take my word against that of Miss Hedda's husband?"

"Perhaps you're right," Gale agreed reluctantly. "Thank you for telling me."

"Not at all, Miss," the old woman said. And she started for the cabin door only to pause and turn when she was a few feet away from it. "Don't forget to ring if you need me," she repeated.

"I won't," Gale promised.

The old woman seemed uncertain, not ready to go yet. Hesitating, she went on, "I hope this voyage will be a lucky one for you and that this film will make you as great a star as Miss Hedda was."

"Thank you."

Maggie Dever's pale face showed confusion. "It's not something I like to bring up, Miss. But it may be you'll hear tales of Miss Hedda's ghost haunting the *Britannia*."

57

Gale felt herself tensing again. Very quietly, she said, "Yes. I have heard those stories."

The maid nodded. "They're true, Miss. I've seen her myself," she said in a troubled voice. And then without waiting for Gale to reply, behaving almost as if it was something she wouldn't discuss, she turned again and hurried out and closed the cabin door after her.

Gale was left standing there filled with mixed emotions. At first she had been terrified on finding Maggie in the cabin thinking that she was some phantom presence. With that situation cleared up she had quickly moved on to a second stage of frustration. The maid's account of the voyage on which her aunt vanished was startling and possibly revealed some of the long-concealed facts. And now Maggie had left her almost as terrified as she'd been in the beginning by confirming the existence of her aunt's ghost on board the *Britannia*.

Maggie Dever was a direct link with the past. Gale had not expected to meet anyone among the ship's staff who had known her aunt. It had been such a long while. But she saw now that some of these people remained with a ship all their working lives. This veteran maid was an example.

At the same time she knew the old woman might be given to fantasy. The disappearance of Hedda Grant had become a legend and it was not unlikely that Maggie Dever might have elaborated on the facts over the years and come to see hidden meanings in what were ordinary happenings. It would be wise not to become too concerned over what the veteran maid had told her. Still!

She turned and went across to the dresser preparatory to changing for the evening. Studying herself in the glass she compared her features with those of the smiling picture of her aunt still prominently displayed there. She could not deny there was a likeness but again she was conscious of the glacial quality of Hedda Grant's smile. Her coldness was evident in this large photograph. Gale considered the maid's reference to having seen her aunt's apparition and again put this down to the old woman's probable enjoyment of sensation. If others had seen Hedda's ghost she was not going to be left out.

The blue-jacketed script of the screenplay was on the dresser near her aunt's portrait. Now Gale picked it up and noted the credits on the inside cover. The name of Jack Henderson meant something to her now and he was given the by-line for the screen adaptation of the story. She flipped quickly through the bulky script that contained Jack's version of her aunt's disappearance. He had chosen to treat it as a murder case but he had also made it clear that his was a fictional treatment and he believed the facts were quite different. But he had made it clear he thought someone had murdered Hedda.

Gale put the bulky script down again. At least she had made a friend she could count on in Jack. And she certainly hadn't many aboard the *Britannia*. Steve Benson had given the impression of friendship but she knew him well enough by reputation not to depend on the handsome star. He had been married and divorced three times and was known for his weakness for any new pretty face. She didn't want to be listed as his latest conquest. At the same time she couldn't snub him since he was co-starring in the film and probably could be helpful to her during the actual shooting of the movie.

With a sigh she began to slip off her afternoon dress before taking a shower and changing into her evening things. Within a short time she was getting into the green velvet cocktail dress she had chosen to wear at dinner. Then she sat down before the dresser mirror and carefully completed her make-up. She wanted to look her best on this first night of the voyage.

She had a broad white shawl with woven silver strands which she took with her as a wrap in case the weather improved and she should go out on deck before returning to her cabin. Then she made her way along the corridor, following the signs to the first class dining salon.

As Jack had told her, it was immense and royally decorated. A smiling headwaiter greeted her by name and informed her she was to be seated at the Captain's table. He led her across the vast dining salon and she realised how empty the old liner must be because of the small number of tables occupied. Only a quarter of the big room was being used. An orchestra played dinner music sedately on a platform at one end of the large dining salon. She followed the headwaiter to the Captain's table which was filled except for the seat waiting for her. Mervin Hawley, the producer-director stood up and came and gave her a warm greeting. The veteran of many Hollywood films was in black tie and dinner jacket as was Steve Benson and the other men at the captain's table. Hawley introduced her around with a special moment for the

Captain, a small, grey-haired reserved man, with a shy smile.

"This is Captain Redmore," the producer said affably. "We are all in his hands until the picture is finished."

"I should say it was you who had the responsibility," Captain Redmore said in his modest way.

The big, florid Hawley chuckled and said, "We'll not argue about it, Captain." And then to her, "You're to sit beside me, Gale."

She found herself seated between the producer and Steve Benson and wryly wondered if the flirtatious leading man had arranged this for his own pleasure. From the moment she had arrived at the table Jane Fair, who was seated almost directly across from her, had ignored her and concentrated on talking to an abashed Jack Henderson who was on the brunette star's left. Jack looked boyish and appealing in his dinner jacket and at the first opportunity flashed her a smile. Jane caught this and demanded his attention with renewed energy.

Steve Benson turned to Gale with a knowing smile. "You see how fate throws us together?"

"I'm much impressed," she said with a faint smile.

"You shouldn't make light of such things," he said in his bantering way. "I knew from the first moment we met we were destined to play major roles in each other's futures."

Gale looked at him demurely. "Before the cameras of course."

The classic profile showed hurt at this. "Must you be so mundane?" the leading man wanted to know.

The food was delicious and Gale gave her major attention to her meal only replying politely to whatever Mervin Hawley or Steve Benson might have to say to her but not attempting to prolong any discussion. She allowed her eyes to wander to the other tables where minor players and the crew were seated. At one of these tables she spotted the thin, crabbed Francois Mailet. The elderly make-up artist seemed aloof from the others around him, and like herself, concentrating on his food.

The orchestra played all through the dinner hour. The lilting dinner music added charm to the occasion and matched the elegance of the walnut panelling and giant tapestries that lined the walls of the dining-room. The ornate crystal chandelier ensconced in a dome-like recession in the high ceiling cast a soft glow on the scene giving it all an old-world grandeur.

Mervin Hawley bent close to her. "I would like to bid on some of these tapestries when the ship is dismantled," he said in a low voice.

She stared up at one of the beautifully woven patterns with some dismay. "They seem so right where they are! But of course they will have to be taken down. Why do they have to tear this beautiful old ship apart?"

The white-haired director smiled. "The *Britannia* has outlived her era," he said. "Not even the smaller shipping lines could find a place for her and make her pay today."

"It is rather sad just the same," Gale said.

"She is a grand old lady," Mervin Hawley agreed. And turning to the Captain he asked, "How long have you been in charge of this ship, Captain?"

"Twelve years," Captain Redmore told him.

The producer nodded. "Then you came aboard long after Hedda Grant's disappearance."

"Years after," the Captain agreed. "There were still some of the hands on her who had been aboard when it happened. I imagine there are still a few. But a very few. Of course the legend was in full bloom by the time I became master."

Mervin Hawley showed interest. "Have you any theories as to what happened to her, Captain?"

He shrugged. "Beyond the fact she found a watery grave in this sector of the Atlantic it's anyone's guess. Nearly every voyage someone comes to me and offers me their version of a reconstruction of the events. I must confess I find none of them convincing."

"I'd say Hedda's vanishing was the most noteworthy event in the *Britannia*'s history," Mervin Hawley said. "So it seems fitting that her last voyage should be dedicated to a filmisation of the story."

Captain Redmore nodded solemnly. "I am glad the ship will be recorded on film. It makes this final trip more endurable to know the *Britannia* will live again in your picture."

Gale stole a glance at Jack and saw that the vivacious Jane Fair was still continuing to monopolise him. She found it amusing that the Hollywood star should vent her jealousy in this manner and felt sorry for the poor young screen writer.

At last the meal came to an end and

Steve Benson firmly took control of her. "There is immediate dancing in the First Class Nightclub," he informed her. "As your leading man I insist on the first dance."

Gale cast an appealing eye in the direction of Jack but saw he was already up from the table and on the way to the nightclub with Jane Fair on his arm. It seemed she had no intention of letting him go. So Gale allowed the determined Steve to escort her.

The nightclub was connected with the dining-room by a short corridor and was not quite so large as the other room. But it was just as ornately decorated. Tables set at intervals on an elevated area surrounding three quarters of a sunken dance floor. At the other end of the club the orchestra were seated on a stand. They were already playing and she noted they were the same musicians who had performed the dinner music augmented by several other players. The dance floor had wood inlaid in the pattern of a giant star and there were already a few couples dancing.

As soon as they had found a table and ordered Steve took her out on the floor. He was an excellent dancer and she enjoyed the music. He smiled down at her and said,

"You count yourself lucky we have such smooth weather even if it is foggy. Legs have been broken on this floor in rough weather."

Her eyes widened. "You don't mean it?"

"I saw it happen once to an elderly gent who persisted in doing a foxtrot while a big blow was on. On that trip there were few made the dining-room and in most of the public rooms the crew had to tie the furniture down."

"You make it sound terrifying!"

The leading man laughed. "I'm telling you what an Atlantic storm can do to a ship even as large as this."

"We're not likely to see anything like that happen," she protested as they made their way around the floor.

He looked sceptical. "I don't know. It can be rough enough along the coast. And in the last few years we've had more spring and summer storms."

She smiled up at him. "I refuse to be frightened."

His eyes met hers. "Even by Hedda's ghost?"

Her smile wavered. "That is something else again," she said.

The music ended and they went back to their table. Now she had a chance to take in her surroundings and saw that Jane Fair and Jack were seated at a table on the opposite side of the ballroom. A long table at which several other people were seated including Mervin Hawley.

Within a short time the veteran director came striding over to where they were sitting and with a smile for Steve Benson said, "I'm going to steal your girl, Steve."

The leading man stood with a pained look. "You leave me desolate," he mourned.

When the big, white-haired man took her on the floor he said, "Steve is a card. Don't pay too much attention to any pretty things he may say to you."

She smiled up at the director. "I've been warned. And I know the various Hollywood characters by reputation even though it is my first experience of working with top names."

Hawley led her well to the spirited music. "You deserve the break if your test means anything. And you'd never have gotten it if I hadn't decided to do Hedda's story."

"What made you decide to do it?"

"I've had it on my mind for years. I guess hearing this old liner was to be scrapped brought it up again. It seemed like the last chance to tell the story in its real setting. And then your agent came to me about you."

She smiled. "I'm beginning to wonder if that was a mistake. I've been subjected to so much publicity. It will be hard to live up to it."

Mervin Hawley's florid face registered confidence. "I'll get a fine performance from you," he said. "Even though we have a few doubters on board."

With a knowing look she suggested, "Jane Fair?"

"How did you know?" he sounded surprised.

"She hasn't gone out of her way to hide her displeasure at my being the lead," Gale pointed out.

"Don't worry about her," Hawley said, his face shadowing. "She came to me with a complicated plan to take over your part and have you do the minor role I have Kate Paxton playing. I told her not to bother me or I'd replace her." He paused. "Do you know Kate?"

"I've just been formally introduced to her."

"Talk to her when you can," he advised. "She's a fine actress and was a friend of your aunt's. She's bitter about not being a star any longer but she's taken it better than I expected. Another thing, she was a passenger on this ship at the time Hedda vanished."

"That's odd," Gale frowned. "So were you."

"That's right," the big man said. "But it wasn't so odd. Most of us had been working on a picture overseas and were returning on the *Britannia*. Your aunt had just finished the London film and took it as well. As a matter of fact I danced with her on this very floor the night she disappeared."

"Was she in a good mood? Did she seem happy?"

The big man shrugged. "Happy enough. She'd been drinking a lot as usual. It was hard to tell about Hedda in those last days. She put on a good front."

The orchestra finished playing. They applauded and then started across the floor and up the stairs to Gale's table. She said, "Things had been turning out badly for her, hadn't they?"

He nodded. "Yes. She was slipping in her career and Jerry Hall, her husband, had been showing signs of wanting to leave her."

Gale gave him a sharp side glance. "Were you and Hedda very good friends?"

He looked uneasy. "I think I was one of her best friends. Why?"

"Do you think she would resent me playing her in the film? She never liked my mother. Refused to give her parts in any of her pictures."

"I know all about that," the director agreed. "I don't know how Hedda would feel about you. I should think she'd be glad to have anyone keep her name alive. But then you could never be sure about her. She was a twisted personality." He took her back to the table where Steve Benson was lingering over his drink and after thanking them both returned to his own party. The handsome leading man glanced at her peevishly. "What did Hawley want?" he asked.

"To dance," she said with mild surprise. "What did you think?"

"He never dances unless he has something to discuss with somebody," Steve Benson informed her. "He was probably trying to find out if you'd heard out about Jane's plotting and reassure you."

"That could be it," she admitted. "He did touch on the subject."

"I told you," Steve said and with a knowing smile. "Time for us to dance again."

Steve kept her busy on the floor until

fairly late in the evening. Then Jack escaped from Jane Fair's clutches leaving her with Mervin Hawley. He came over to Gale and asked for a dance and they remained together for the rest of the evening. When they were tired of dancing he led her out to the deck. The fog had lifted but the night was cool. She was glad to have her white shawl. They leaned against the railing and he pointed out a long line of distant lights.

"That's Long Island we're leaving behind," he informed her. "By tomorrow we'll be out of sight of land."

"And the picture will begin," she said.

"Weather permitting," he agreed. "How do you feel about it all?"

"More than a little scared," she admitted. "What did Jane Fair have to tell you?"

He laughed. "That woman talks mostly about herself and it's strictly a non-stop performance."

Gale raised her eyebrows. "She didn't get around to me?"

He nodded. "She did give you a brief mention. It is her theory you won't manage in your aunt's role and she'll have to take over."

"So she still has hopes. What did you say?"

His eyes twinkled. "I assured her she was wrong. I said I had written the part for you."

"Which wasn't exactly the truth!"

"It would have been if I'd met you before I did it," he said with a sudden tenderness in his eyes. And then he surprised her by taking her in his arms for a kiss. When he let her go he looked vaguely embarrassed and said, "Don't take that as a Steve Benson approach. I really mean it! I like you!"

Gale offered him no arguments but looked up into his pleasant boyish face with her own eyes shining. At least something nice had happened to her at last. She let him see her to her cabin door where they had a final goodnight kiss. So she entered the suite feeling happier and less tense than anytime since she'd been on the old ship.

Switching on the light she closed the door and locked it. Then she went across to the dresser and stood staring at her smiling reflection. At that instant all thought of ghosts and the terror she had known since boarding the *Britannia* had left her. But it was not to be that way for long. She glanced down to look at the script which she had left on the dresser

73

wanting to read Jack's name on it again. And it wasn't there!

With a frown she searched the dresser top quickly but it had vanished. Then she looked on the floor and saw it. It was torn to bits in a heap with a strip of glistening wet seaweed across it!

Chapter Four

All at once everything in the room was changed for her. The eerie sight of the destroyed film script with seaweed on it and the small puddle of water surrounding had the same effect on her as a ghostly accusing finger. It was as if Hedda Grant had emerged from her ocean grave to wreak her anger on the filmscript and leave it there in tatters.

Gale stared at it with loathing on her pretty face. Then she forced herself to bend down and gather up the torn wet pieces and drop them in the waste basket. When she picked up the slippery bit of seaweed she was filled with fear and repugnance. Having cleaned up the floor she rushed into the bathroom and washed her hands. Then she slowly came back to the bedroom of the suite and stared about her with apprehensive eyes.

Who had done this insane, awful thing? Who had been vindictive enough to enter her suite and deliberately destroy her copy of the script? Someone who had access to keys that would fit the cabin's door. Her first thought was of Maggie Dever but she dismissed the maid as a suspect at once. She hadn't the guile for such an act. So it must be one of the film company who hated her enough to plan this vandalism to frighten her and discourage her from continuing in the starring role.

Her first suspect would be the attractive Jane Fair. But she couldn't remember whether the star had still been in the ballroom when she left or not. If she had left early then she must have somehow gained access to the cabin and done this dreadful thing. But what about the seaweed and the puddle of sea water? A chill ran through her as she speculated on these items. Once more she was tempted to consider a vision of a spectral Hedda Grant risen from the ocean crypt she had slept in so long.

One thing was certain, her peace of mind had been neatly destroyed again. She knew she would have difficulty sleeping and dreaded switching the room to darkness. She compromised by leaving on a small clamp-on reading light that was attached to the top of her bed. Settling down on the pillow she tried to somehow put this unpleasantness out of her mind and get some rest. But it was not all that easy. With the quiet of the night she was more aware of the slight roll of the great liner and the creaking of its plates as it made its way through the dark ocean.

Once she thought she heard someone moving about in the living-room and sat up quickly, fear marring her lovely face, but after a few minutes of strict attention to every sound she decided it had been merely a complaining plate as the weary old *Britannia* ploughed along to her destination off Cape Cod.

When Gale did finally fall asleep it was a deep, dreamless one and she did not awake until morning. And then only when Maggie Dever came briskly into the cabin with tea on a tray. Gale sat up on an elbow still not completely awake.

The maid's pale face wore a smile. "Good morning to you, Miss. I have your tea. I thought you might be needed for an early call. It is a fine sunny morning."

"We're not to begin work until the afternoon," she said. "But I'm glad you've wakened me anyway." She sat up to take the cup of tea Maggie Dever was pouring for her.

"I'll be serving your breakfast in here as well," the old woman said. "If you'll just tell me what you'd be liking."

Gale told her what her usual breakfast requirements were and just as Maggie was about to leave she asked her, "Were you in the cabin during the late evening last night?"

The old woman smiled. "I did drop by for a moment to see if everything was all right."

"And was it?"

"So far as I could tell," the old woman said. "You were in the bathroom. I heard the water running. I rapped on the door and you didn't answer. So I left."

"Thank you," Gale said quietly. And she didn't bother to tell the old woman it hadn't been her in the bathroom. At least this explained part of what had gone on last night. Whoever had entered the cabin had been caught there by Maggie's sudden entrance and taken refuge in the bathroom. It hardly sounded like the action of a spectre.

Maggie returned with her breakfast later and then Gale washed and put on a warm woollen suit and made her way out to the deck. It was a pleasant surprise, the sun had come out and it was really warm now. All around her stretched the placid silver of the ocean as the fine old liner flowed along its course. There were no other craft in view and when she gazed down at the water she found it a terrifyingly long distance below.

She strolled towards the rear of the *Britannia* and then climbed the steps to the higher observation deck. It was where she had first met Jack Henderson and she hoped she might by some stroke of good fortune find him there again. As soon as she reached the top of the steps she saw him. But he wasn't alone. Mervin Hawley was standing talking earnestly to him. Both men were in sport clothes and hatless.

She approached them with a smile. "Everyone seems to have risen early this morning!"

Mervin Hawley gave her a jovial glance. "I don't know about writers," he said. "But I've always been an early morning riser. I've already gotten things set up for the scene we're going to shoot on the forward deck this afternoon."

This reminded her and she said, "I'm afraid I'll need a new script. Mine has gotten damaged."

The big man's florid face showed mild surprise but he asked no questions. Instead he said, "I'll have one sent around to your cabin."

Jack now spoke up. "I've been telling

Mervin about Joseph Holland. He didn't notice the item concerning his escape from the asylum in the paper."

The white-haired veteran director frowned. "I can't imagine how I did come to miss it. Probably the extra pressure of getting ready to sail."

Gale said, "Did you know him well?"

"Very well," Mervin Hawley said. "He lived in Hollywood for some years. Joe was quite a character. A small man. All nerves!"

"But a genuine talent," Jack Henderson put in. "Or so the critics seem to think."

"He was the sort of genius who always bordered on insanity," the director said with a grim note in his voice. "I wasn't surprised when he finally had to be committed to an asylum."

Gale studied the director closely. "Wasn't he on this ship when my aunt vanished?"

Again the big man looked uncomfortable. "Yes. I remember Hedda telling me about the row they had. She thought he had done an awful job on her portrait."

Jack Henderson smiled. "It was different. It marked the beginning of his eccentric period when he painted everything pale and willowy."

"Hedda didn't fancy herself that way," Mervin Hawley said. "And I didn't blame her."

"What was Joseph Holland's attitude?"

"He ranted around the ship like the wild man he was," Hawley snorted with disgust. "Joe would never admit being in the wrong. And I think by that time he was so unstable mentally that he wasn't responsible."

Gale said, "I wonder what he's like today?"

"He must still be insane enough to warrant restraint," Hawley said. "The thing these days is to get mental patients out if they are half-well. I'd judge he is a bad case." He turned to Jack again. "I have to be moving on. But we'll have a script conference after dinner tonight. Keep it in mind."

"I will," Jack promised.

The director turned to her with a smile. "I'll see you both on the set this afternoon. Captain Redmore says we can count on this fine weather for a few days and I want to shoot all the exteriors I can."

He vanished down the stairs leaving them alone. Jack indicated some empty deck chairs across from where they were standing and said, "We may as well make ourselves comfortable."

She smiled as they crossed the deck. "I was almost certain I'd find you up here."

"Less chance of running into some of our associates," he observed with a look of amusement on his boyish face. She decided that his small moustache didn't suit him as they did some men. When they were comfortably settled in the deck chairs she leaned towards him and confided. "I have a new mystery to tell you."

He showed interest. "Go ahead."

She gave him a careful account of the events of the previous night trying to get in every detail. Then she moved on to Maggie Dever's mention of someone being in the bathroom when she entered. "It certainly wasn't me," Gale said.

Jack glanced at her thoughtfully. "It sounds as if Hedda returned from the dead and tore the script up in a jealous rage."

Gale nodded. "That's what they want me to think. The seaweed and the puddle of water! It's just too obvious!"

"But who?" he asked. "Who do you suspect?"

Her eyes met his. "What time did Jane leave the ballroom?"

He considered. "Before us. I'm sure of it. I turned her over to Hawley and they both left before we did. I saw them go while we were dancing and then Steve Benson left right after."

"Then it could have been Jane."

"I can't see it," Jack said. "I don't think she has the brains for such an artistic touch. And where would she get a key to your cabin?"

"There are probably sources we haven't even guessed," she said. "I know the maid has one. And the steward. And who knows who else!"

"Sort of community property," Jack said glumly. "Why couldn't it have been this maid? You say she was a great fan of your aunt's. Maybe she resents you taking her place."

"I don't think so. She isn't the type."

"But there was that odour of what you took to be Hedda's perfume in the cabin at the same time you discovered Maggie there," Jack pointed out. "Doesn't it strike you she might have got her hands on some similar perfume and done that as well?"

Gale looked confused. "I don't think so!" She slumped back in the deck chair. "I may as well be honest! I don't know!"

"Did she mention the perfume?"

"She didn't seem to notice it. By the time we'd finished talking there was only a trace of it in the room."

"But it had to get there some way," Jack persisted. "Unless you want to blame everything on the spirits."

She saw the teasing smile on his face. "It's no joke," she reminded him. "It's a serious business for me. Almost as if my aunt had returned and was making her presence known to me. Warning me against going ahead with this picture."

Jack at once became serious. "You're not going to let them scare you off, I hope."

"No," she said definitely. "I'm not going to let them do that." For in spite of what Jack had said about Jane's not having the brains for the incident she privately felt the brunette was the guilty one. And she was determined to fight it out.

She was even more convinced when she saw the look of annoyed surprise on Jane Fair's perfect oval face when she came on the set carrying her new script. She was sure Jane had expected her to arrive without one and ask Hawley for a new copy there. It was the only sign the brunette star gave of being aware of her presence, she at once sulkily resumed a study of her own script.

The forward section of A Deck was a hive of activity as she took the canvas chair with her name on it. Mervin Hawley stood far front where his cameramen had set up and discussed the angles from which the scene was to be taken. More than one camera would shoot the action and then the exposed footage from each would be neatly selected and spliced together by the editor to make an interesting scene. Giant reflectors had been installed at strategic points to make the most of the available sunlight. Sound men were locating microphones and making tests. Jack Henderson stood against the railing at the far side of the deck from her in discussion with another man whom she recognised as being the assistant director.

Steve Benson sat with Jane Fair, both of the stars wore dark glasses as did Gale and most of the crew as the bright sunlight reflected on the water was hard on the eyes. Gale was quite a distance from her co-stars and while she waited for a call a slim dark-haired woman came and sank down in the canvas chair beside her. The slim woman's sun glasses did not completely conceal the beauty of her face. Gale recognised her at once as Kate Paxton the former star whom Mervin Hawley had suggested she get to know.

Kate Paxton said, "Aren't they ever

going to be ready? It's a quarter-hour past call now."

Gale smiled. "I guess shipboard living induces a leisurely pace."

"It seems so," Kate Paxton said and she took a pack of cigarettes from her pocket and lit one. She watched the cameramen with lazy interest. "I wonder what the public would think if they watched the filming of some of our intimate love scenes," she said. "With not less than fifty people besides the lovers being involved and stolidly looking on."

"Was it always this way?"

"Much simpler in the silent days they tell me," the former star said. And with a hint of acid in her tone, "I don't go back quite that far."

Gale was apologetic. "I didn't mean to suggest you did."

Unexpectedly Kate Paxton smiled and reaching over patted her arm. "Sorry. I haven't any right to be so touchy," she said. "To be truthful I can remember the silent days although I was only a teenager then. And I want you to know I'm on your side."

"Thank you," Gale said sincerely.

Kate Paxton nodded across to Jane Fair and Steve Benson. "I wouldn't trust either of those two if I were you," she warned in a low voice. "Some of the company are bent on causing a feud. I don't go along with that. It nearly always works out badly for everyone and we end up with a rotten picture."

"I'm glad someone feels the way you do."

Kate Paxton's mouth set in a cynical line. "Jane came to me with a generous proposition and I was immediately suspicious. I know that one too well to trust her." The slim woman smiled. "Your aunt and I were friends in the old days. That is why I'm especially interested in you and this picture." She paused. "I knew your mother too."

Gale returned her smile. "Then there's nothing I can tell you about my aunt."

"Not a thing," Kate said dryly. "She was a fine actress before she began to drink too much. I enjoyed working with her. But we were never close personal friends and I always felt she treated your mother rotten."

"It's a long while ago now," Gale said. "I guess I shouldn't hold a grudge. And anyway I'm getting this big chance through Hedda."

"So you are," the older actress agreed. "And I'll bet it would make her wild if she was alive to know about it."

Gale was about to ask her some more questions about her aunt when Francois Mailet, the thin little make-up man came forward to her. "Miss Bond," he said, in his high voice, "I would like to work on you now. We're using the first cabin on the right."

She excused herself from Kate Paxton and followed the little man in to be made up. He had a very completely fitted cabin for the purpose and a girl assistant whom he kept busy with a flood of sharp orders. Gale could tell he was not an easy person to work for and would win no prizes for a good disposition.

He glared at her in the chair. "We haven't met since the other night," he observed tartly.

"I have seen you," she said. "You were at the other table."

His pinched face was grim. "We are not on the same social level with you stars," he said acidly.

"I hadn't thought of that," she said quietly.

The eyes behind the heavy glasses gave her a keen scrutiny. Then he announced, "Mervin Hawley asks the impossible. He wants me to make you look like your aunt."

88

Gale was seated in the chair, a white towel over her hair and another draped over her body. She smiled, "I'm afraid there isn't much resemblance aside from our complexions."

Francois Mailet shook his head. "You do not even have the same type of complexion. You lack Hedda Grant's beauty in every respect. To make you look like her is to ask for the impossible."

"It's a fictional character," she said. "Only suggested by her."

"Indeed," the little man snapped. "There will be little of Hedda in all this. But I will do what I can." He went to work quickly but with the dedicated manner of a true artist. "You have fatigue lines at the eyes," he sputtered. "And at your age! What do you expect to look like when you're forty? A hag?"

"I haven't had much rest since I've been on the ship," she said. "I suppose it shows."

"No rest?" the little man was sarcastic. "Why? You worry about not being a great enough artist to fill your aunt's shoes?"

"Not exactly," she said. "Things have been happening. Unpleasant things."

Francois continued to apply her make-up. "Your conscience bothers you because you know all this is a travesty. A mockery of your aunt."

"I think you are being unfair," she protested.

"And I am not interested in your opinions," the make-up man snapped back. "Also I cannot complete your make-up if you continue to chatter incessantly."

Gale took the hint and said no more. Francois' assistant returned and he again vented his anger on the poor girl. He took another five minutes to finish Gale's make-up and she was glad when he drew away the towels and told her she could leave.

When she got out of the chair she paused a moment to study herself in the mirror and gave a gasp of delighted surprise. "You're wonderful!" she exclaimed. And she meant it for the dour little man had worked a marvellous transformation in her appearance with his deft magic. She looked more glamorous and a lot harder. In fact she appeared remarkably like the Hedda Grant whose portrait sat on her dresser.

The dour little Francois showed a hint of satisfaction on his pinched face. "I have done a little," he agreed reluctantly.

She smiled at him. "I know Mervin Hawley will be pleased."

"Mervin Hawley is always pleased by my work," Francois said with the hint of a sneer. "That is why I am here."

Gale left the cabin and went back to her chair. Kate Paxton gave her a surprised look. "What a transformation! Now you seem the double of Hedda as I remember her."

"Francois is a wonderful make-up man," Gale said with a smile.

"But what a strange little person!" Kate Paxton said with a shake of her head. "I've met him before on Hawley's pictures. He's so ugly. And a regular recluse! No one sees him after the day's work is over."

Their conversation was interrupted by the actual work on the film beginning. They were doing a scene in which Steve, playing Hedda's husband, came down from the upper deck and met an actress friend of his wife, played by Jane. She twits him about Hedda's affair with the Chief Officer and he pretends not to believe her.

Later, Steve would question Kate Paxton in the role of Hedda's maid and there was a final dramatic scene between the jealous husband and Hedda, played by Gale, in which she tries to convince him she has been just flirting with the Chief Officer to satisfy her ego as she has with many other men.

It was an exacting business getting the final arrangements for shooting made. The big Mervin Hawley patiently journeyed between cast and crew until all was ready. Then Steve and Jane took their places on the upper deck and the cameras began to roll. The scene between the two went well and Gale found herself admiring Jane Fair's crisp handling of lines if she didn't care for her as a person. Steve also was getting everything possible from his role of the husband. Then without warning he stumbled in his lines and the veteran director roared, "Cut!" and it all became a shambles.

Kate Paxton groaned and in a voice just loud enough for Gale to hear said, "Steve has these days. I hope it doesn't go on forever."

As it turned out it did happen again. Mervin Hawley handled the situation with his usual tact but Gale could feel the tension grow on the set. And she could see that Jane Fair was seething with inward anger and liable to explode at any time and at anyone. She began to worry about her own scene and hoped the brunette girl would leave the set before she began to work. And she did. Gale did not have a chance to do her scene until late in the afternoon.

Hawley was approving of her make-up. "You look exactly right," he said. "Now play it as you did in the test."

Steve Benson did not offer her too much help in his playing of the husband. By this time he seemed weary and listless in his approach to the part. But they did manage to get one good scene between them done before it was time to call it a day.

Hawley congratulated her. "A fine beginning," he said. "Tomorrow we will really get down to your scenes."

"I'll work on my lines tonight," she promised.

"Do that," the veteran director said. "And I want you to come to the theatre at nine sharp. I am having a special screening for the cast."

She left the set and hurried back to her own room where she removed her make-up and stretched out on the bed to rest. Although she had only acted a short time the tension of being on the set all afternoon had proven exhausting. She woke in time to change for dinner and Maggie Dever came by to look after her bed before she left for the dining salon.

The veteran maid was all smiles. "I went out and watched you from the sidelines this afternoon, Miss Bond," she said. "You looked the exact image of Hedda Grant. It fair gave me the creeps."

Gale laughed. "Give the make-up man credit for that."

"It brought back those other days," the old woman said mournfully. "It's hard to believe so many are gone. And this is to be our last voyage." With a sigh she went on into the bedroom.

Gale again joined the Captain's table for dinner. It was much like the night before. Jane Fair still managed to avoid looking her way and Steve Benson continued to pay her embarrassing attention. Only with Mervin Hawley did she feel at ease since she was too far away from Jack to carry on any conversation with him.

The veteran director confided in her. "I have a surprise for you all tonight. I managed to get the print of one of Hedda Grant's last films and I'm going to run it for the company. It will give you a better idea of what she was like than any directions I can ever offer."

Gale didn't know whether she cared to see the film or not. Under the circumstances it would be a scary experience for her. She had caught glimpses of several old Hedda Grant films on television but the circumstances had been quite different then. Here, on this old ship, with its chilling record of Hedda's ghostly appearances she was not certain she cared to see her aunt's image on the screen.

On the other hand she didn't want to offend the eminent director. And he was clearly excited about the prospect of showing the film. There was also truth in his statement that it would help her to mould her performance of the late Hedda Grant. All in all she would have to attend the screening.

She found Jack as soon as they left the table and confided her woes in him. He was sympathetic. "I don't blame you for not looking forward to it," he told her as they stood outside on A Deck. "I wish I could be there with you to hold your hand but Hawley wants some new scenes for the script and I've got to work on them tonight."

Gale made a pouting face. "Now I really am blue. I was sure I could at least count on you."

"I'll come by as soon as I can," he promised. And he gave her a kiss to seal the bargain.

Feeling somewhat better Gale reported at the movie theatre amidships at nine o'clock. Most of the others were already there and she chose a seat in the last row by herself. If she was to study the performance she didn't want to be interrupted. Down front Mervin Hawley rose to make a few brief comments. Then he waved for the show to begin. The lights in the small theatre were turned off and Gale sat in the darkness to watch the Hedda Grant vehicle unwind on the screen.

It was a drab love story and she thought her aunt looked gaunt in it. There was a hint of the famous fire that had made her a star but only a hint. Sometimes Gale felt the troubled eyes of Hedda Grant stared directly at her from the screen. And once she had the eerie feeling that the long dead woman might be going to come straight forward to her. She sat, caught up in her study of the other woman's screen technique and hardly aware of her surroundings. Then she came alert with a start as she had the feeling there was someone directly behind her. She was about to turn when cold, clammy hands grasped her throat and her head was drawn back. She fought to free herself and uttered a low choking sound which she was sure no one would hear.

Chapter Five

Gale fought to escape and to hold on to her consciousness. But as the cold clammy hands continued to press on her throat she knew that she soon would black out. She could not breathe and still the relentless pressure of those ghostly hands increased. From the screen she was dimly aware of Hedda Grant screaming imprecations and it seemed that these were directed at her and the hands closing off her breath were those of the long dead woman.

Her head reeled and the pain from her throat became unendurable. She let herself go limp. She could struggle no more. Drifting through a vague black universe with no sound and no light she was suddenly aware of urgent whispering from a long distance off. Then the whispering became louder and more insistent. She recognised the voice of the whisperer. It was Jack!

Wearily she turned to the sound and opened her eyes to see his shadowed face bending over her in the semidarkness of the theatre. "Gale! What happened?" he asked in that low hoarse voice.

She was aware of her paining throat and that in the distance the film still continued but everything else seemed to move like slow motion in her sluggish mind. Her hand reached up to her throat and she straightened in the seat to stare at him with terror mirrored in her pretty face as memory returned. "Someone tried to choke me!" she said in a low voice. "Someone came up behind the seat and grasped my throat!"

Jack stared at her with a look that bordered on doubt. "Are you sure?"

"Yes. My throat is still aching. Didn't you see anyone?"

He shook his head. "When I came in your head was slumped forward and you were unconscious. I thought you must have fainted."

"No!" She touched her hand to her injured throat. "Get me out of here!" she begged.

He quietly helped her to her feet and gave her support and they went out one of the rear exits so as not to disturb the rest of the audience. As soon as Gale got a breath of the fresh sea air she felt a great deal better. She leaned weakly against the rail and looked up at the troubled Jack.

"Someone intended to murder me just now," she said in a solemn voice. "If you hadn't come along and scared them off they probably would have."

He frowned. "It doesn't seem possible!"

"Look at my neck," she said. "There must still be marks."

He studied her throat. "There are some red spots," he admitted. "They could be bruises. Does it feel any better? The ship is carrying no doctor this trip but there is a nurse. We could call her."

"No need," she said. "I'll be all right. Give me a moment."

"Who could it be?" he asked. "Who would attack you like that?"

She looked at him, her face pale. "They were strong hands."

"I'd imagine that," he observed grimly. "I wonder who left the auditorium and went around back to creep up on you."

As he finished speaking the actress Kate Paxton came out on the deck. She gave them a surprised glance. "Sorry! I didn't mean to intrude!" And she seemed about to turn and go back in.

Gale stopped her by stepping forward and asking, "Did you just leave the screening?"

Kate Paxton, looking very much the great lady in a long black gown, with a sparkling diamond necklace and a bracelet to match, nodded. "Yes. The picture is almost over. I've seen it a half-dozen times."

"Did either Jane Fair or Steve leave the theatre before you?" Gale wanted to know.

The older actress showed some amazement. "As a matter of fact they did. At least three-quarters of an hour ago. So did a lot of others. And I don't see how Mervin can blame them. It is a dreadfully dull film!"

Gale turned to Jack with a knowing look. "You see. It could be almost anyone."

Kate Paxton frowned. "Is something wrong?"

"Very much so," Jack said. "Someone tried to choke Gale."

The fading screen beauty gasped. "Someone what?"

"It's true," Gale told her. "I was seated at the rear of the theatre and someone came up from behind and tried to throttle me. They probably would have if Jack hadn't arrived."

Kate Paxton's eyes narrowed. "Dreadful! You must complain to Mervin Hawley at once. The culprit must be found! Who knows which of us on this lonely old ship might be next?"

Jack said, "I have an idea Gale is the only one who is in danger."

The older actress looked startled. "How can you say that? If a maniac is at large on this nearly deserted ship we're all easy targets!"

Gale gave her a meaning look as she said quietly, "Jack is suggesting I was attacked for a special reason. Because someone wants me out of the way."

Kate stared at her in silence for a moment. "You can't mean that Jane had anything to do with it?"

"I don't know," Gale said. "She has been trying to get Hawley to remove me from the lead. Maybe she decided this would be a surer way."

"No!" Kate dismissed the suggestion. "That is too far-fetched. It has to be somebody else. One of the crew or some of the film company workers. There are plenty of suspects on board."

"Far too many," Gale agreed. "I think I'll go to my room."

Kate nodded. "I'll see Mervin now and send him there to talk to you about this business."

"I don't think it will do any good to worry him," Gale protested.

Kate was firm. "I'm thinking of the

101

safety of us all. Don't you agree, Jack?"

He was slow in replying. Then he said, "Yes. I guess you are right."

They left a badly worried Kate Paxton to break the news of the assault on Gale to Mervin Hawley as soon as the movie ended. Meanwhile they walked along the deserted open deck in the direction of cabin A20. Gale still felt ill and shaken and leaned heavily on Jack's arm as they made their way in the darkness and quiet. The old liner rocked gently as she moved through the night at a low speed. You could feel the vibration of the great engines far below and hear the regular wash of the waves as she ploughed along.

Gale hoped that Kate Paxton would not raise too much of a fuss. But she realised the screen actress was right. They were all in danger from this unknown menace. Better that they make some attempt to solve this mystery at once. And could it be solved? Or were they dealing with a true phantom? Had it been Hedda's hands that had reached out in the darkness of the theatre and grasped her throat in their clammy coldness?

They went inside and walked the dimly lit corridor to the entrance of cabin A20. Gale switched on the light and then went into the bathroom to give some attention to her aching throat. When she returned to the living-room of the suite Jack was pacing up and down with a wan look on his boyish face. He turned to greet her. "I've been thinking," he said. "It has to be Steve acting for Jane or maybe Jane herself."

She smiled wryly and sank into an easy chair. "You're willing to accept that at last?"

"I have to," he said, with a frustrated sweep of his hand. "There is no one else with a motive."

"I disagree," she said. "It could be someone who admired Hedda so much the thought of my playing her on the screen maddens them. Or it could be the person who originally was responsible for her vanishing, ready to have history repeat itself."

He frowned. "There are quite a few people on board who made that last voyage with her."

"I think we should make a list and consider each of them carefully with respect to motive and temperament."

"Hawley is among them," Jack pointed out.

"I wouldn't even exclude him."

He looked startled. "This is getting to be

madness. Next you'll not want to exclude me."

She nodded seriously. "Probably I shouldn't. Nor ought I to rule out the ghost theory. A lot of people will attest to the fact that Hedda's does frequent the *Britannia*. So perhaps it is her unhappy spirit that is trying to avenge itself on me."

Jack stared at her with incredulous eyes. "You must be joking!"

Gale knew that in a grim fashion she was. Yet it was not entirely black humour she was indulging herself in. There was more to it than that. There had been the episode of the phantom perfume, the torn script with the seawater and seaweed soaking it and now the bony fingers that had circled her throat in the darkness. No wonder the ghost of the vanished screen actress had become so real to her. No wonder she was almost ready to accept the story that Hedda regularly left her watery resting place to haunt the decks of the doomed *Britannia*.

Pushing aside these grisly thoughts she said, "I have a feeling there is more still to come."

"There had better not be!" Jack said angrily. Before he could continue there was a knock on the cabin door. He went over and opened it and Mervin Hawley came in quickly.

The big man's florid face wore a look of distress. "What is this I hear about someone attacking you in the theatre, Gale?"

"It's true," she said.

"I thought Kate must be exaggerating," the veteran director said in a shocked voice.

"I discovered her in a faint," Jack assured him. "And you can still see the marks on her throat if you examine it closely."

Hawley stared at Gale. "You're sure you didn't see who it was?"

"I had no chance," she said. "There wasn't any warning. Just the hands on my throat."

The screen director stood in silence for a moment. Then looking from one to the other he said in a tight voice, "Of course you realise what this means? It means we have a madman aboard."

"Or a madwoman," Gale said quietly.

"I'm willing to bet on my first guess," the director said. He looked sheepish. "In fact I have evidence to back me up. Captain Redmore received an urgent message from the New York authorities tonight. He advised me at once. At my suggestion he agreed to keep the message private." The big man sighed. "It seems that my judgement in the matter has been proven wrong."

Jack said, "What are you talking about?"

Gale was sure she already knew. With a sober glance at the director she said, "It's Joseph Holland, isn't it?"

His eyes opened wide. "How did you guess?"

"It fits," she said.

Mervin Hawley sighed. "Well, I'm sorry to say you're right. The New York police seem to think Holland got on board this ship some way and is hiding out on her right this minute. According to them he's completely demented and dangerous if cornered. It's not a certainty he's here, mind you. But there's a strong chance of it."

"In view of what has happened I'd say every chance," Jack said.

The director looked forlorn. "It means a setback for us. As soon as the word gets out we'll have a lot of frightened people aboard. It'll ruin our working schedule and it may all be for nothing. He may not have come aboard at all."

"Still you plan to tell the others now?" Gale asked.

"I haven't much choice," Hawley said with a shrug. "Kate already knows and she's bound to spread the word. I've told both of you."

"More importantly you're endangering the lives of the others if you don't give them a warning," Jack said.

The director's florid face was a study in misery. "I'll have the Captain post the news on the bulletin board tomorrow. I only hope it doesn't start a panic."

Gale gave him a sharp glance. "Don't you think the ship should be given an intensive search at once?"

"It's under way right now," the director said. "But it's a pretty hopeless task. On a ship as big as this and with such a small crew and passenger list there are just too many places to hide."

"They'll not find him," was Gale's prediction.

"I'm inclined to agree," Hawley said. "So we'll go on with fear spreading through the ship's company and my crowd until nothing is being done properly. I tell you there is a jinx on this picture."

Gale smiled wanly. "Didn't you worry about that when you first thought about the story? I think I would have."

The director gave her a wary glance.

"I'm not a superstitious man, Miss Bond." He lapsed into the formal use of her name in his apparent anger.

"I'd say that was fortunate," she said lightly.

The director frowned. "I should have the nurse look at you."

"I'm all right," she promised him.

He hesitated. "Well, it seems there is nothing more I can do here. I'll keep in touch with the Captain. And if he turns up Joseph Holland I'll let you know."

Gale rose to see him to the door. As he opened it, she said, "Do you think Holland was responsible for my aunt's death?"

The big man scowled. "I've never thought about it," he said. "I have no theories."

After he'd gone she glanced at Jack. The young writer looked upset. He said, "What do you make of him?"

"I haven't decided," she said quietly. "I think he knows a lot more about what happened to my aunt than he wants to let on."

Jack came over to her with a sigh. "We can thank our lucky stars that maniac didn't finish you off in the theatre."

"I don't think it was Joseph Holland who attacked me," she said.

The young man stared at her. "You don't?"

"No. I have strong doubts whether he is actually on board or not. As I understood the message from the authorities in New York, they only presumed he might be on this ship. I'd say the chances were against it."

"That takes us right back to where we started," he complained.

"I realise that," she said. "But we should face the truth. And that is this rumour of an escaped Holland being on the ship will come as a welcome relief to the real would-be murderer. It will also offer the guilty person leeway to act and blame the crime or crimes on Holland."

"You're so certain," he said. "You must have some idea who you suspect."

"I'm sorry," she said. "I don't. And now you must go. I'm very tired."

They kissed goodnight and she closed and locked the cabin door. If Joseph Holland should be on the *Britannia* she couldn't picture herself as being afraid of him. But she was more than terrified by the unknown that threatened her, whether it was some jealous rival, the possessor of a long guilty conscience or the actual ghost of Hedda Grant come back to destroy her. On this sombre reflection she went to bed.

Whether it was the official notice on the

bulletin board or the fact that bad news spreads fast by any means it did not take long for everyone on board the ship to learn about the escaped lunatic, Joseph Holland, the next morning. By the time Gale reported on the set for the morning's work it seemed that the news was on everyone's tongue.

When Francois Mailet put her in the chair to be made up he regarded her with a sour expression. "So someone tried to murder you last night," he said in his weird, high voice.

She felt embarrassed. "Who told you that?"

"The ship is full of it," the little man said as he began work. "I'd think you'd be afraid to have me make you look like Hedda with Joseph Holland lurking in the shadows somewhere waiting to kill you."

"Do you think he was the one who killed Hedda?"

"Shouldn't be much doubt of that," the little man said fussily as he applied eye shadow on her eyes. "He went mad not long after she disappeared. Guilty conscience I'd call it."

"And now you think he's come back to commit the crime again with me as the victim," she said carefully.

"Didn't he try to choke you in the theatre?"

"Someone did."

"Huh!" The sour make-up man sounded disgusted. "Maybe you want to make a mystery of it? Blame it on someone else?"

"I want to be sure Joseph Holland is actually on board and guilty before I go shouting around he's the one who tried to murder me."

Francois Mailet removed the towel from her head and then the one from her body. "You're ready," he snapped. "And I think you're right. I doubt if it was Joseph Holland who came after you."

She looked at the wizened, angry face. "Oh? Why do you agree?"

"Because I don't think he'd bother with you," the little man said enjoying his venom. "You're too ordinary except when I make you up to look like Hedda. She was a real beauty."

Gale managed a smile. "I'll try to remember that when I'm alone on dark nights. It will give me comfort."

When she left the make-up man's cabin and went to the forward deck the technicians were going through the same elaborate preparations as on the previous day. Perhaps half the time was spent getting

111

ready to take scenes. Director Mervin Hawley was everywhere at once shouting directions to electricians, indicating where sound men should lay their cables and discussing the light and camera angles with his head technicians. Meanwhile the acting members of the company sat about morosely in the canvas chairs bearing their names waiting to be called.

Gale took her usual chair beside Kate Paxton and found the older actress in a bad mood. It seemed the former star had been involved in some sort of argument with the dour Francois Mailet.

"That Francois!" she complained to Gale. "He tries to make me look like a hag. I told him so this morning. I let him know I had looked after my own make-up for years and I wasn't going to let him ruin my face."

Gale smiled ruefully. "He's very difficult. Certainly he doesn't go out of his way to offer me compliments."

"Neurotic little tyrant!" Kate Paxton said angrily. "I intend to complain to Mervin about him," she stared at her closely. "I don't think he's even bothered to do you as well as usual."

"He seemed very upset about the news of Joseph Holland being on board," Gale said.

"So I gathered," Kate said. "Well, it doesn't take much to jar his type. I've had my fill of him. It's bad enough that we may have a lunatic lurking in the shadows ready to attack any one of us as he did you last night."

"I'm not convinced it was Joseph Holland who choked me," Gale said frankly.

Kate raised her eyebrows and glanced across where Jane and Steve Benson were seated. The two co-stars of the production were busily engaged in conversation and paying no attention to the confusion going on around them.

Then the former star gave Gale a questioning glance. "You think it may have had something to do with them?"

Gale was saved from voicing an opinion when Director Mervin Hawley came over to her. The big man was wearing sun glasses like nearly everyone else and his checked sports shirt was open at the neck.

"Are you feeling well enough to work?" he asked her solicitously.

"I'm perfectly all right," she assured him, removing her glasses.

He looked pleased. "Fine!" he said. "Then we'll start the scene between you and Steve again. Where you meet on deck and have the argument."

It marked the beginning of a long and difficult day. Gale was in front of the cameras all morning and she began to understand how Mervin Hawley had built his outstanding reputation in the film business. He was a perfectionist. Time and again he repeated each segment of her argument scene with Steve Benson.

By lunch time she was commencing to feel tired. She had a short period of rest then and she and Jack had their light meal in the dining-room at a suitably remote table for two. He brought her up to date on the search for Joseph Holland.

"Captain Redmore has had a party of three men searching constantly," he said, "And he hasn't found a sign of Holland. I'm beginning to wonder if he is on the ship."

She smiled faintly. "I told you my opinion in the beginning."

"You don't think so."

"I doubt it very much. I can understand the New York police contacting the ship since they are also investigating every possibility."

Jack sat back in his chair. "I think Captain Redmore is about ready to halt the search. He feels it is useless."

"I can't say that I blame him."

114

"How about a swim after you finish work this afternoon?" Jack asked with a smile. "There is plenty of time before dinner."

She was mildly surprised at his suggestion. "There is no deck pool that I've seen," she said.

"They had one for their cruises but it has been removed," Jack told her. "However, there is still a big indoor pool and gymnasium way down below. I was down there this morning and I think it would be refreshing and fun to take a dip in it at the end of the day."

"Why not?" she smiled.

"Pick up your bathing suit on your way back to the set," he suggested. "Then we can go directly down to the pool as soon as you finish. There are dressing areas for men and women down there and loads of lockers. We'll not be crowded."

So she stopped by the cabin and got her swim suit and put it in a large cloth bag she always carried with her on the set. The afternoon session was longer than the morning one and just as tiring. Again Steve Benson started to look haggard at about four o'clock and began making errors in his lines. This required additional retakes. Jane Fair remained on the sidelines to watch them and Gale could almost feel the brunette's cold eyes fixed on her.

When Mervin Hawley called a halt at five o'clock Gale drew a sigh of relief. She quickly cleaned off her make-up and joined a waiting Jack Henderson. The young writer was in a happy mood at the prospect of their swim.

As they descended endless stairways and went along dim corridors at each lower level she began to wonder just where the pool was located. "It must be well below the water line of the ship," she suggested as they walked along a narrow dark area.

He laughed. "Probably," he said. "I hadn't thought about it. Anyway it's right ahead through that swinging door."

The pool and gymnasium were a revelation to Gale. She had not guessed there were such facilities. The ceiling was high, the area around the pool of a dull marble material and the pool itself was long and fairly narrow. The big space was gloomy and lighted by fluorescent lights but it was apparent many of them were no longer working and so the light was poor. But it was a salt water pool and apparently available for their private use.

"It's completely deserted down here," she said with a glance at Jack. Her voice echoing in the silence of the vaulted pool area.

"Be thankful for that," he told her. "Jane and Steve come down occasionally I'm told. Let's hope we aren't bothered by them now." He indicated an opening at the other end of the gymnasium. "That's the entrance to the ladies' dressing room. I won't be a minute. I'll join you here at the pool."

Gale followed his directions as he went the opposite way to his own dressing room. As soon as she left him she felt a trifle nervous in the murky light of the remote area. The dressing room was even darker and as she changed in the shadowed room she lost no time. She was anxious to get back to the pool and Jack's company. The attack on her the previous night had left its mark of terror. She fastened the second strap of her white one-piece suit and slipped on her bathing cap as she hurried out to the pool again.

She stood by the chrome railing of the ladder leading into the water and glanced about the big gloomy area hoping that he might appear any minute. But he didn't. She stood there shivering and growing increasingly nervous. And impulsively she decided she would feel safer in the water than waiting there. Carefully she made her way down the ladder and into the tepid water of the heated pool. A moment later she struck out and began to swim. At once she relaxed.

A moment later there was a splash in the water and she knew Jack had joined her in the pool. She shouted to him and turned to find him but he had dived below the surface and was remaining there, probably to surprise her by bobbing up at her side. She had just reached this conclusion when she heard a distant moan and turned shocked eyes in the direction from which it had reached her. What she saw made her cry out with alarm. Jack, in his bathing suit, was staggering forward to the pool. As she watched with an agony of fear she saw the blood streaming down his temple and with a glazed look in her direction he collapsed by the pool side!

But someone was in the pool with her!

Her horror was complete as strong hands grasped her body and drew her roughly under the water.

Chapter Six

Inexorably Gale was pulled below the surface of the pool by those unknown powerful hands. She struggled to free herself once she had recovered from the numbing horror that had first come over her when she saw Jack collapsing and felt the vice-like grip of her attacker. Her lungs were bursting for air as she fought to free herself and save herself from being drowned. As consciousness began to leave her and her mind began to wander she saw the hard smiling face of Hedda Grant before her and had the thought that the long dead beauty had returned to drag her down to a watery death such as she had met thirty years before.

It was her last conscious thought. The next thing she was aware of was a familiar male voice calling her name in a rather frantic manner. Slowly she opened her eyes to look up into the distraught face of leading man, Steve Benson. Another man in ship's uniform knelt beside him looking anxiously over the actor's shoulder. Wearily she came to the conclusion the ship's

119

officer was a much younger man and had a nicer face even if he hadn't the classic profile of the screen star. She knew it wasn't really relevant but at the moment it was the only thought that came to mind.

Steve Benson lifted her up a little. "You are alive after all!" he exclaimed.

"Alive?" she asked in a small vague voice. Looking around she saw she was stretched out on the marble area beside the pool. And then her pretty face contorted with horror as it all came back to her. "Jack! Where is Jack?"

"Sitting on a bench over there," Steve said patiently. "He's still a bit out of it. He's had a bad blow on the head."

Weak and nauseated as she was she now sat up on her own. She saw Jack with his head in his hands seated on the distant bench. "What happened?" she asked looking at the other two men with wild eyes. "Who was in the pool with me?"

Steve and the ship's officer exchanged glances. Then the young officer said mildly, "You were alone in the pool when I came in. I thought I had heard a scream. You surfaced and were near the rail. I managed to grab you and drag you out."

"But there was someone in the pool with

me!" Gale insisted. "Someone who tried to drown me!"

Again the two men looked at each other. Steve Benson answered her now. "I arrived after Chief Howard dragged you out. You were unconscious. For a moment I was sure you were finished."

With the actor's help she struggled to her feet and rushed across to Jack. The young writer's temple was covered with blood and he looked up at her with his eyes still dazed. "Turned out to be a bad idea," he murmured. "Sorry."

She sat by him and with her hand on his shoulder asked, "Who did it, Jack? Who hit you? You must have seen them."

"No," he said with a sigh, his head in his hands again. "Happened too suddenly. Didn't see!"

Steve Benson had come over to them. "You'd better go up and see the nurse," he said. "Both of you." Turning to the officer he said, "You'll show them the way, Chief?"

The young officer nodded. "Yes, sir."

"Better pick up their clothes first and take them along," the leading man said. And while they waited for the officer to do this, he gave his attention to them again. "It looks as if that escaped lunatic must

121

have caught up with you two. As I remember it Joe Holland was a strong swimmer."

Gale didn't bother to discuss it with him. She was much too upset to care at the moment. All she wanted was to see that Jack received prompt medical care. When the ship's officer returned with their things over his arm they followed him to a deck above where the matronly ship's nurse had her office.

She spent some time cleaning up the wound at Jack's left temple. "I wish we had a doctor this trip," she worried. "It's a bad blow and there's always the danger of concussion."

Jack was now well enough to offer a weak smile. "Patch me up and I'll be satisfied," he said. "I had no bad headache or anything of that kind."

"It could be serious," the nurse insisted. "At the very least you must take it easy for a few days."

Gale was standing by him. "Whoever struck you must have followed me into the pool," she told him.

His eyes widened with concern. It seemed he was realising for the first time that she had also been in serious danger. "Followed you into the pool?" he repeated.

"Yes. I never did see who it was. You came staggering out and I knew it couldn't be you. Before I could make any fuss someone grabbed me and pulled me under and kept me there until I nearly drowned."

Jack frowned. "Then it's the same old pattern," he said. "It was really you they were after. I was struck down merely because I stood in the way."

Gale nodded. She had changed into her clothes in the bathroom just off the nurse's office. "It begins to look that way."

His boyish face was grave. "They had an ideal chance. With me out of the way and you down there alone it's a wonder they didn't finish the job."

"They would have if that ship's officer hadn't come along. Whoever it was must have heard him and been frightened away."

"That's the way it seems."

Jack gave her a sharp look. "Where did Steve Benson figure in it?"

"He arrived soon afterward. He and the young officer were bending over me when I came to."

"Steve must have come down for a swim," Jack went on thoughtfully. "He was wearing a dressing gown over his bathing suit, wasn't he?"

"I think so," she ventured. "Yes, I'm certain of it. A red dressing gown. Silk."

The nurse finished placing a taped bandage over the injured temple. "You come back and see me in the morning, young man," she admonished. "Before that if you have any more pain. I can always have wireless put out a call for medical help."

Jack got up with a grim smile. "I'll be all right," he assured her. "I've had worse blows than that."

The nurse gave him some sleeping tablets and suggested he go to his cabin and rest for a few hours. Then she allowed them to leave. Against Gale's wishes he insisted on seeing her to her cabin door.

He seemed troubled as if there was something on his mind that he hadn't mentioned. Now he said, "I'm still thinking about Steve showing up down there so soon after everything happened."

She stared up at his pale face, the bandage prominent at his temple. "But you spoke of him and Jane often going there for a swim."

"I know that," he admitted. "And I guess everyone will blame Joseph Holland for what happened. They'll be more certain than ever the lunatic is aboard."

"So?"

"I'm trying to remember," he said. "Did

you notice if Steve's body or his hair were damp?"

She frowned. "I can't say that I did."

"He says he came down after the ship's officer found you." Jack paused and gave her a significant look. "But suppose he was there earlier. That he was the one who struck me and then dived in the pool and tried to drown you. He could have heard the ship's officer coming and made his escape by another way, thrown on his dressing gown and pretended to have just reached the scene."

"You're right," she said, awed by his expert reconstruction of what might have happened. "And to be sure all we'd have to know is whether he was wet or dry. And we were both too upset to take notice."

"He could have counted on that," Jack said grimly. "Perhaps that ship's officer noticed."

"We could find him and ask," she suggested.

Suddenly Jack looked gloomy. "I don't know whether it would help. Steve could always say he'd just taken a shower before coming down to the pool."

She showed scepticism. "And came down without towelling himself?"

"Why not? It would give him a fine alibi."

"You think he might actually be guilty?"

Jack smiled wanly at her. "You were the one suspicious of him and Jane a short time ago. Have you changed your mind?"

"Not exactly. She was sitting glaring at me all afternoon while I was working. I know she wants the Hedda Grant role but would she go as far?"

"She might. Especially if she was able to talk Steve Benson into being her accomplice. It still seems odd that he should show up there at that exact time."

"It could be merely a coincidence," she pointed out.

"I know," he sighed.

"What can we do about it?"

"Nothing I guess," Jack said glumly. "We'll just have to wait and let things reveal themselves." He paused. "My head is beginning to ache now. I guess I'd better try a couple of those sleeping tablets. That means I'll be missing dinner. You watch yourself."

"I may stay in my cabin," she said.

"I would most of the time," he agreed. "Not that I'm sure it's all that safe."

He left her and she went inside. It was getting late and she knew if she were going in to dinner she would soon have to dress. The living-room had a fancy imitation fireplace with an electric log that could be turned on. Its fittings were all metal and the fireplace itself was finished in a metallic tile. A hearth rounded out in front of it with a low iron railing with sharp spiked points at intervals. She now stood by the fireplace her foot on the railing and her arm on the mantel. She rested her head on her arm as she lingered there deep in thought. All at once there was a knock on her cabin door. She went over and opened it to see Captain Redmore standing outside.

"May I intrude on you for a moment?" the diminutive Captain asked politely.

"Of course," she said, standing back for him to enter. He came in, gold-braided hat in hand, looking impressive in his neat uniform in spite of his small stature. "Please sit down, Miss Bond," he said in his grave way. "It has just been reported to me that you had a narrow escape at the pool."

"That is so," she admitted, taking one of the easy chairs.

He twirled his cap slowly in his hands, plainly agitated. "This is a very serious business," he said.

"I suppose you'll renew your search for Joseph Holland," Gale said.

"Yes. That follows." He paused. "You're

sure that the sight of Mr. Henderson collapsing by the pool and his apparent injuries didn't throw you into a panic?"

She frowned. "I was upset, of course."

He seemed embarrassed. "I mean you're sure you didn't imagine all the rest. Someone else being in the pool and trying to drown you and all that."

Gale tried to hold back her anger but she was surprised at the Captain's tone and his suggestion that her story of being attacked in the pool was the result of hysteria on her part.

She said, "It all happened exactly as I described it."

He raised a placating hand. "I'm not questioning your word. I just want to be certain what did take place. The story you tell gives the incident a quite different colour. You realise that?"

"In what way?"

He spread his hands. "It is possible to picture a frightened and demented Joseph Holland having taken refuge in the men's dressing room and becoming panicky at Mr. Henderson's entrance there. It would be a natural result that he should pick up a wrench left there by a workman and approach the young man and strike him. After that he'd likely run for safety in a new hiding place somewhere deep in the bowels of the ship. I can't picture him remaining to leap in the pool and attempting to drown you. It doesn't have a logical sequence. He would have no motive for doing it."

She looked at the little Captain directly. "You don't really think Joseph Holland is on the *Britannia* do you?"

He hesitated a moment before replying. Then he said, "I didn't up until this happened. Now I'm not so sure."

"I wouldn't allow it to change my views," she said. "I don't believe it was him who caused the trouble at the pool."

"If your story is correct in detail I would agree," Captain Redmore said.

"It is correct, Captain," she said solemnly.

His lined face looked troubled. "Then that would indicate something of quite another sort."

"Yes?"

"We have a murderer among us. Someone bent on killing you."

She nodded. "That seems to be what I am faced with."

"Any suggestion as to who it might be?"

"I wish I had," she said sincerely. "I think it all goes back to my signing to do this story and play the role based on the life of my aunt. There was too much blatant publicity. Apparently someone wants to see me die as my aunt did."

"The shadow of Hedda Grant's disappearance has hung over the *Britannia* for most of her time," Captain Redmore said frowning down at his gold-braided hat. "It had become a legend by the time I took over as master."

"It would seem that the mystery will never be solved," Gale said.

"I have come to accept that," the Captain agreed. "Though I briefly entertained the idea the truth might come out on this final voyage. We have so many people who knew your aunt on board, so many who were on the *Britannia* the night she vanished."

"Instead it seems that history might merely repeat itself with me as the victim." She paused. "You have heard all the tales about Hedda Grant being seen in various parts of the ship by many people in the years since her death. Do you believe in ghosts, Captain?"

He smiled thinly. "Sailors are a notoriously superstitious lot. There is so much mystery to the sea it is almost unavoidable. I have known men who swear they have seen the *Flying Dutchman* in full sail."

Gale said, "I'm beginning to wonder if I don't accept the ghost theory myself. All the things that have happened to me since I came on this voyage hint at the malicious avenging acts of one person. A person we know met her death in this part of the Atlantic three decades ago. A person determined to prevent me from gaining any fame by impersonating her."

"You are referring to your aunt, Hedda Grant."

"She fits the motives for these acts so perfectly," Gale went on with a serious expression on her lovely young face. "One wonders if that bitter, angry spirit has somehow transcended death to leave her imprint on this ship. To return and hound me to a fate similar to hers."

"I do not see the enemy as a ghost but as a living person," Captain Redmore said. "Perhaps someone closely associated with your aunt. Someone who loved her or knew her well. There are quite a few on board."

"And Joseph Holland could be counted one of them. Perhaps the search should continue for your mad artist after all. I am told that he and she had a quarrel the night of her disappearance."

"I will keep looking for Holland," he promised. "There is much of the ship to be covered yet. In the meantime I ask that you exercise extreme care. Keep with other people as much as possible. Don't go anywhere alone. Especially after dark."

He left after she promised to obey his suggestion. After some consideration she decided she would go to dinner after all. It would be less lonesome than eating in her cabin by herself. The orchestra was playing in the big dining salon when she went in but there was little else to indicate any gaiety in the group assembled there.

Mervin Hawley rose to help her be seated beside him as usual but the director's florid face wore a brooding look. Jack did not show up at the table at all and the others seemed strangely subdued. Especially Jane Fair and Steve Benson. Jane left the table before dessert was served and Steve had little to offer in his bantering talk.

Mervin Hawley said quietly, "There is a sort of strange mood settling over the entire ship. It looks bad for us."

"I hope it doesn't turn out that way," she said.

"Maybe I was a fool to attempt this picture," the director said heavily. "I'm also to blame for dragging you into the mess and any danger that should be involved."

She smiled ruefully. "My agent was quite enthusiastic about the project."

"True," the big white-haired man said. "But it was I who began it all. I can blame no one else." He paused.

"Something about the *Britannia* seemed to draw me back to her. When I read of her being due to be scrapped I got this idea."

"It may still work out well enough."

He frowned. "With that killer Joseph Holland on board," he said, "I'm afraid not. Unless he is found there will be more trouble. Perhaps more attempts on your life."

"I mean to be very careful," she said.

"Please do," the director begged her. "We've made a good beginning on the film. It shouldn't take us long if we don't panic. Then we can head back for port."

The Captain engaged Mervin Hawley in a discussion of the weather prospects and the advisability of changing their course. A small blow had been predicted for the general area although it might change direction. As the two debated what their action in the matter should be she found herself left with only Steve Benson to talk to. She had a strange feeling toward the handsome leading man after what had happened down at the pool. She couldn't help a lingering suspicion of him.

He gave her a concerned glance. "Are you feeling better now?"

"I'm all right."

"How is Jack? I see he didn't make it for dinner."

"He's still feeling badly," she said. "He's resting. The nurse gave him some sleeping tablets."

"After what has been happening we could all do with a few," Steve Benson said bitterly. "I thought you were a goner this afternoon."

She shrugged. "I'm more durable than you'd guess." She decided if he was putting on a show of innocence for her benefit he was proving himself an excellent actor.

As they finished dinner, he suggested, "Let me escort you to your cabin since Jack isn't here to do the honours."

She decided to avail herself of the offer. She had given her promise to the Captain that she wouldn't go about the ship alone and more especially after dark when the danger of attack from some hidden enemy would be increased. She still wasn't certain about Steve Benson or his motives but she doubted if he would make any move against her if they were seen leaving the dining salon in each other's company.

As they made their way to the door they passed one of the other tables and she saw the grumpy make-up artist Francois Mailet was seated at it. When they were almost by the table the little man glanced up and seeing them the eyes behind the thick glasses showed scorn. Francois had little regard for actors. He considered them mere puppets for him to decorate for their roles.

At the door Steve suggested, "Let's stop by the ballroom for a drink and dance. It's going to be a long evening."

She hesitated. She didn't really want to go nor did she want to appear unfriendly. She said, "For just a short time then."

There were not as many other people in the ballroom as on the previous evening they had been there. Mostly they were from among the crew of the film company. Neither Mervin Hawley nor any of the other principals of the cast were there. In a way Gale was glad. She felt less conspicuous among these comparative strangers. The orchestra was playing as gaily as before and no one would have thought from the scene in the ballroom the *Britannia* was a doomed ship plagued by violence and an escaped madman.

Steve ordered and then they danced a little. Gale was not in the mood for a light-hearted evening and she noticed that Steve's manner was also nervous and strained. They returned to their table again and she led the way in small talk preparatory to suggesting they leave.

She smiled across the table at Steve. "I noticed Francois in the dining salon," she said. "From the way he glared at us I'd say we weren't his favourite people."

The leading man shook his head. "Nothing personal in that. Francois just happens to hate all actors."

"Have you worked with him before?"

"A couple of times," Steve said. "He's regarded as one of the best in his line since he showed up in Hollywood."

She registered surprise. "I thought he was an old-timer."

"He is. But I believe he spent most of his early years in Germany. From there he moved on to Paris and eventually London and Hollywood. He's only been working in Hollywood less than ten years."

"He spoke of my aunt as if he knew her well."

"He probably did," the man with the classic profile reminded her. "You know

Hedda worked frequently in France and London."

"I'd forgotten for a moment," she admitted.

Steve regarded her with a faint smile. "I've been thinking," he said. "If Hawley intended to type-cast when he set you for the role of Hedda he was miles off. I knew her. And she wasn't at all like you."

"I'm sure he's aware of that," she said. "He's using me because I am her blood relative. That helped with the publicity. And Francois can at least make me look like her."

"He does suggest Hedda in you," Steve agreed. "But you are the exact opposite from her. You are a mild person, she was a kind of tigress."

"So I've been told."

"You're probably like your mother," he said. "It was the talk of Hollywood that Hedda wouldn't let your mother play even a walk-on in any of her films."

"Mother was aware of that," Gale said with a sad smile. "She didn't want to work with Hedda."

"And here you wind up impersonating the wicked lady," the leading man said with a thin smile. "For Hedda was a very wicked lady you know."

"So I've heard."

"She had many more enemies than friends," Steve reminisced. "I was one of her crowd even though I was a lot younger. I remember Joe Holland and all the rest of them."

"What was Holland like then?"

"Thin, intense type," he said. "Madly in love with Hedda and wanted to marry her. She made fun of him. The irony was she really loved her husband. And Jerry Hall didn't care anything about her other than the money he could make off her. He married her at the time when she was earning top money and at the time she vanished and was on the down grade he was ready to ask for a divorce."

"You really think that?"

He nodded. "I'm certain of it. He told me so. Of course when Hedda disappeared that solved everything. And he died shortly after." The actor paused. "I sometimes wonder why Mervin Hawley wanted to make this picture. I guess you can put it down to a desire for revenge."

She arched an eyebrow. "Revenge?"

"Yes. He wanted to hire Hedda for a series of films when she was a name and she refused him. I think that is why he decided to have you play her and tell the story of her life in his own way."

"Jack Henderson's way," she reminded him. "He created the script."

"On Hawley's suggestion," Steve said. "And I think the idea of having a murderer involved is especially intriguing. No one put Hedda's death down as murder. We all felt she was a suicide. But Hawley apparently has a different slant on the mystery."

"Do you think that is because he knows something no one else has guessed?"

"It's a possibility," the actor said warily.

She sat back in her chair. "It's getting late. I really must go."

She was a little surprised that the handsome leading man did not attempt to persuade her to stay longer. But he seemed quite willing to leave. Again she felt a certain tension in him that seemed foreign to his usual self.

They left the ballroom and went out on the open deck. It was dark now and there were no stars. There was a high wind and the waves were larger and the old liner rolled and groaned like the weary veteran she was. Gale took hold of the railing and braced herself as she took a deep breath.

"There could be a storm on the way," she said. "I heard the Captain mention it at dinner."

"I thought it was supposed to veer away

139

from us," Steve said.

"Perhaps," she agreed. "This might be just the fringe of it."

She stared out at the rough white-capped waves again and waited for his reply. But there was none. After a moment she turned to him and to her surprise she found that he was gone. He had left her without a word! Frowning she turned to scan the deck in the other direction. There was no one in sight.

At first she was merely annoyed. And then she began to realise she was by herself on the lonely open deck and some distance from her cabin and she started to feel vaguely nervous. Steve had deserted her at the moment she needed him most. She began to make her way along the empty, slightly heaving deck. Passing close to a lifeboat with its canvas cover in place she listened to it creaking with the ship's motion and for a panicky moment thought she saw a movement from the concealment of the canvas. Then she realised it was her imagination. Summoning every ounce of her sorely tried courage she went forward in the darkness.

She had gone perhaps twenty feet further when she saw the figure appear and slowly move towards her. A figure still some distance off but coming her way so they must inevitably meet. Her heart began to pound fiercely and she tried to fight the trembling that had taken hold of her slim young body. For the figure gliding up to her was the one she had so often heard described. Every detail was correct, the pillbox hat, the flowing veil, the fashionably long suit. It had to be Hedda's ghost!

Chapter Seven

As soon as she identified the figure with her long dead aunt, Gale came to a halt. The wind howled mournfully and the *Britannia* swayed with its gusts. The apparition drew closer to her and still she stood there frozen with fear. Then from somewhere distant on the deck there came a clatter as if a bucket had joggled from its resting place and fallen to roll mindlessly back and forth with the ship's motion.

It broke the spell for Gale and with a frightened scream she turned and began running along the heaving deck. She heard the sound of footsteps coming after her at a rapid pace and knew the spectre was following her. Sobbing and panting for breath she headed for a door that would give her access to the inner corridor and allow her to escape this phantom and make her way to her own cabin safely.

The footsteps behind her seemed nearer and she fairly hurled herself at a nearby door and grasping its handle pulled it open and dashed inside. The inner corridor was gloomy and ill-lighted but not so frightening as the deck. Especially the deck with the ghostly figure of Hedda holding forth.

Now she ran along the corridor with its thick carpeting not daring to look behind. Hoping that she might have left the apparition out there in the lonely wind and darkness. Fumbling in her purse for her key she quickly unlocked the door of cabin A20 and let herself in. She was gasping for breath and she felt ill. Hurriedly she switched on the lights and then carefully locked the door and leaned against it listening with her back to the living-room of the cabin. Pressing her ear close to the metal door she waited for the sound of footsteps outside. Footsteps to herald the advent of the spectre of the *Britannia*!

So she had seen it at last! But now in the safety of her cabin she was ready to doubt the evidence of her own eyes. Her thoughts moved rapidly. And she thought she knew why Steve Benson had been so nervous and why he had left her without warning. Probably he had arranged with Jane Fair to impersonate the ghost and so reduce her to a state of nerves she would no longer be able to continue her role in the film. It was typical of the two she thought bitterly. And she blamed herself for so easily falling for Steve's deceit.

If Jack hadn't been recovering from the attack on him he would have been there to protect her and with a feeling of warmth she realised how much she had come to depend on the pleasant young writer. She had a strong desire to go to his cabin and tell him what a frightening experience she had undergone. But she knew he had taken sleeping tablets and would probably still be resting.

Realising what a difficult day she'd suffered and still shaken by the night's eerie encounter she decided she would take one of the several remaining sleeping pills she had. If she was going to do any kind of decent work in the morning it was essential that she get a good night's rest. And she was bound to let the tricky Steve Benson and the jealous Jane see that they had not frightened her as they'd hoped.

Taking the events of the evening together with what had happened at the pool she was ready to accuse Steve Benson of the main role in the plot against her. She would see the Captain in the morning and tell him of her suspicions. She was sure he was a sincere and conscientious man and would delve into the matter until it was

144

settled one way or another.

With this thought she prepared for bed. The wind had risen higher and the rolling of the venerable liner was more evident in the cabin than ever before. She wondered what it would be like in the morning and doubted that Mervin Hawley would be able to do any scenes if the storm grew worse. Certain she wouldn't be likely to sleep without some sedative she took the sleeping pill as planned and slid between the sheets.

Because it was of potent strength its action was swift. Despite the creaking of the complaining old vessel she quickly dropped off into a deep sleep. It was not, however, a sleep bereft of dreams. Much of the day's unhappy atmosphere permeated her sleeping visions. A pale, macabre Hedda Grant rose out of the pool and seizing her drew her down in the green depths of the water. She fought at first and then relaxed and let the soothing water flow into her nose and mouth and fill her lungs, and she was at rest in the arms of the sinister Hedda. The screen star's lips fixed in a malevolent smile and she crooned a sing-song whining dirge in her ear.

A great sadness came over Gale for she

knew now she would be the ghostly Hedda's prisoner for all time. Drifting in the green bottomless ocean, cut off from all she loved. Lost to Jack Henderson! Great masses of seaweed encircled them as they drifted along and she felt their cold slippery touch like giant eels slithering by. She turned to her aunt to beg for her freedom, to plead to be allowed to leave those silent murky depths and return to the earth where she belonged.

But her frantic pleas fell on deaf ears for now she saw that in spite of the vice-like grip of Hedda's hand the once beautiful actress was pale in death, drifting in the water, her mouth opened in a soundless cry, the face showing a startled expression, the sightless eyes gazing upward. Gale uttered a scream of sheer terror. She was doomed to go on floating beneath the ocean a prisoner of this vengeful corpse for all eternity!

She fought to free herself. And all at once she was choking, she could not breathe! And the water had vanished and now she was in a garden! A garden filled with giant blooming roses. Clusters of the tall lovely flowers greeted her at every turn. At first she was entranced by them and bent to enjoy their fragrance. But then the fragrance became overpowering! She couldn't get her breath! The roses were all around her! She was being suffocated by them. She screamed for help!

Gale sat up in bed and cried out! And in that instant she awakened from her nightmare. But in a sense the nightmare continued in the darkened room for the odour of roses still persisted. It almost sickened her. And as she became more alert she recognised the scent as the one that had filled the room once before. Hedda's scent!

Desperately her fingers sought the pull chain of the small reading lamp attached to her bed. The darkness was more terrifying than she had ever known it to be before. At last she had the chain and the light came on. Even by its dim concentrated glow she was able to see that there was no one in the bedroom. But there was the living-room beyond and the bathroom. Plenty of room for an intruder to find a hiding place.

But this intruder would need no hiding place. Surely a ghost could appear and vanish at will. At least that was what she'd always heard. Now she might soon find out. She remained sitting up in bed staring around with frightened eyes. Then she realised she had been perspiring, thin trickles of perspiration ran down her soft cheeks. The sleeping pill and her nightmare had combined to produce this result.

And she had wakened to a different sort of nightmare. The odour of roses had begun to waft away now as had happened before. Gale knew the ghostly presence must have been very near indeed, the area around the bed had fairly reeked of roses when she'd first sat up. The wind was howling outside and the cabin was swaying more noticeably than when she had gone to bed. Far below she could hear the steady pounding vibration of the engines.

She suddenly felt very small and weak and much in the hands of fate. The sleeping pill still partially clouded her mind and she felt a strong desire to close her eyes again. But she would not dare turn out the light. Let that at least be a barrier between her and the unknown horror that haunted the cabin. She sank back on the pillow with a weary sigh and shut her eyes. In a short time she had fallen into another deep sleep.

It was morning before she woke. And it was Maggie Dever coming in with her tea that ended this sleep of the exhausted. She sat up in bed and gave the old woman a questioning glance.

"What time is it?" she asked.

"Almost nine, Miss," Maggie said with a smile. "I didn't dare hold back your tea a minute longer."

Gale slipped on her dressing gown over her shoulders. "What is it like out?"

Maggie Dever had poured her cup of tea and now handed it to her. "It's still windy and rough, Miss. But not a candle compared to last night's blow. I tell you it was really rough between midnight and dawn."

"I know," Gale said and sipped her tea. "I wonder if they'll be able to do any work on the picture this morning?"

"I much doubt they'll get anything done outside," the old woman said as she stood by the bed. "It's raining a wee bit and the ship is still far from steady."

"I'd better hurry breakfast and be ready just in case," she said.

Maggie Dever nodded. "The usual, Miss?"

"The usual."

The veteran maid seemed ready to leave and then she stared at Gale with an odd expression in her bleary eyes. "What a lovely cameo locket!" she exclaimed.

Gale stared at her blankly. "Cameo locket?"

"The one you're wearing, Miss Bond. I

can tell it's an old piece. I dare say it came down to you through your family."

Gale was now frowning and she glanced down and saw that she indeed had a gold chained and mounted cameo at her throat. A cameo she had never seen before! She stared at it in disbelief and as if to make sure it really existed, took it in her fingers. It was real enough!

"This isn't mine!" she gasped in dull amazement.

"Whoever it belongs to, it looks mighty smart on you," Maggie Dever said with a smile on her gentle, lined face. "I'll be back with your breakfast in a few minutes." And she left her alone.

Gale continued to stare at the locket. There was simply no reasonable explanation as to how it had reached her room and found its way to her neck. She could only guess that while she had lain in a drugged sleep someone had furtively entered in the darkness and slipped the locket around her throat and fastened it.

Someone? She recalled the strong odour of rose perfume that had brought her awake. Had she been visited by a phantom then? A ghostly Hedda Grant who had left this solid token of her midnight call. Gale shivered as a chill of fear went through her small body. Her immediate impulse was to remove the locket. Her hands were on its catch when she changed her mind.

Sanity told her that some living person must be guilty of this action. Someone determined to undermine her will by continued wearing down of her nerves. That someone would be bound to be looking for the locket and if they saw it on her neck they might betray themselves in some manner. For this reason only she made up her mind to go on wearing it through the day.

When Maggie returned with the breakfast she casually asked the old woman, "I don't suppose you can remember the kind of perfume my aunt used? One of the company told me the other day it was very distinctive. I'd like to get some."

The maid's elderly face took on a triumphant smile. "Indeed I do know about it, Miss. In fact one of the last times she was on the *Britannia* she gave me some in a bottle that was nearly empty. I treasured it for ever so long. Mainly because it had been hers. It was a rose perfume, Miss."

"That's what I heard," Gale said quietly. She felt it would be unwise to confide the truth in the old servant.

Maggie furrowed her ancient brow. "It's

a strange thing, Miss. But the other day I came in here and I could have sworn I smelled that perfume in here again. It was that strong I almost expected to see Miss Hedda come out from the bedroom." The old woman paused and sighed. "But it must have been someone else who had been in the room with perfume something like it. It couldn't be Miss Hedda, could it?"

Gale gave her a searching look. "Not unless it was her ghost," she said very quietly. "I believe you mentioned you'd seen it."

The old woman showed fear. "That was only a shadow, Miss. Nothing solid as you might say. Just a fleeting shadow. The poor dear!"

She at once felt sorry for needlessly upsetting the veteran servant about something she could not understand. In order to pass an awkward situation off she said, "I had several guests here the other day. No doubt the perfume belonged to one of them."

"Yes, Miss," the old woman said in a low voice. But her manner had changed and she was unduly subdued. Gale was anxious to finish her breakfast and join the others. She wanted to find out if they'd be working and she also wanted to let as many people as possible see the locket and test their reactions. She became quite thrilled at the idea and for a time forgot the macabre implications of the manner in which it had come to be draped around her neck.

She even picked a dark brown linen suit to match it and suitably show it off. Then she made her way to the corridor and the forward section of the ship. As she walked she was again aware of the old vessel's swaying motion. It was still quite severe.

The company were gathered in the forward lounge. Since it was still raining some, there would be no outside scenes done. And she doubted if they would start on the interiors. Mervin Hawley was standing in the centre of the lounge talking to one of the cameramen when she came in. He nodded and came over to her.

"No company call this morning," he said. "If it calms a little we'll begin work on some of the cabin scenes this afternoon. There are some new pages of script to replace a couple of scenes I didn't like. You can get them from Jack."

"Fine," she said.

The director's florid face showed an interested look. He reached out and took the cameo in his fingers. "That's interesting," he said. "Looks familiar. Where did you get it?"

"A gift from a friend," she said very casually, being careful to keep her eyes fixed on him.

He smiled and let the cameo drop back against her. "It's a good one," he said. "I guess most cameos look alike." And he turned away to resume his talk with the cameraman.

Gale found herself with mixed emotions. The white-haired director who had known Hedda so well had shown a definite interest in the locket and had seemed to recall it. Then he had suddenly changed his mind. Had it been a subtle move to cloak his real feelings? She wondered. The next person she encountered was a sheepish Steve Benson. The classic profile looked slightly green and even though he was dressed in the usual smart sports outfit with a carefully tied cravat he seemed dejected.

"Sorry about last night," he apologised. "I was suddenly taken ill."

She raised her eyebrows. "Was that it?"

He nodded. "Yes. I think it was something I had for dinner plus the rough water. Even though it's calmer now I don't feel much better."

"You should sit down somewhere quietly," she sympathised, at the same time holding the cameo in her fingers so he would be sure to notice it.

He was literally staring at the cameo now but he made no reference to it. Instead, he said, "I hope my leaving you that way didn't upset you. You got back to your cabin safely?"

She offered him a mocking smile. "I must have! Here I am!"

Steve smiled weakly in return. "Yes, of course." He continued to study the cameo. "Jane wasn't able to appear at all this morning. She's really seasick."

"Too bad," Gale said without conviction.

He nodded. "I'll see you later." And he hurried off in the direction of the corridor and she supposed his own cabin.

So that was to be his alibi for deserting her in such a despicable way last night. He had been suddenly taken ill. Well, it would do and the weather was certainly making it appear authentic. But she thought he had behaved in an extremely guilty fashion and he had surely stared at the cameo hard enough whether it meant anything or not.

The business with the cameo was beginning to have all the thrill of a new game for her. She stood near the middle of the large

155

lounge and looked for another person to apply her test to. Seeing a huddled figure in a big easy chair smoking a cigar and reading a paper she made an instant decision and headed for the chair.

It was close to one of the pillars supporting the lounge roof and the man with the cigar glanced up at her with an irritated expression on his pinched face. It was Francois Mailet. He said, "No company call this morning. Don't you know that?"

She smiled. "Yes. I'm just wandering around."

He curled a thin lip as he regarded her with his cigar in hand. "The exuberance of youth!" he said in his odd squeaky voice.

She showed him the cameo. "I've just picked this up," she said in a statement close to the truth. "Do you like it on me?"

"I'm a make-up specialist not a costume advisor," Francois Mailet told her indignantly. "You're wasting your time and mine asking me such a question." He jammed the cigar in his mouth with a fierceness amusing in such a wizened figure and lifted the newspaper again.

Gale moved on. She had gained nothing there except to annoy the little man but then he was always annoyed so she need not fret. She walked the length of the lounge before she saw someone else she felt like talking to. This time it was Kate Paxton who was sitting alone in a chair facing the deck and studying the angry, white-capped waves. "Sit down," she invited Gale with a smile on the faded but still rather lovely face. "Look at those waves! Aren't they magnificent!"

Gale seated herself with a small laugh. "Some of the company don't think so. Jane Fair is too ill to leave her cabin and Steve Benson claims he's been sick in spells ever since last night."

"Weak stomachs to match weak minds!" the former star said with her eyes shining as she watched the rise and fall of the waves. "This is just a big wind not a real storm."

"It's the first time I've seen the sea in this humour," Gale admitted. "I find it awe-inspiring."

"When you've crossed the Atlantic by ship as many times as I have you'll have seen every sort of weather," Kate Paxton said. And then with a pitying glance at her, "But of course you won't. You'll fly when you go to Europe. Soon it will be all giant jet airliners and the luxury of a sea voyage will be traded for a few frantic, crowded hours in the air."

"That seems to be the pattern," Gale admitted. She had become so interested in the conversation with Kate Paxton she had forgotten about the cameo. But now the older woman was staring at it in such an odd fashion that she was at once conscious of it again.

"Where did you get that?" Kate asked indicating the cameo.

"In my cabin. Among my things. Why?" Gale asked innocently.

Kate Paxton's face was a study. "It's like one I saw years ago," she said in a low voice.

"I think this is quite old," Gale said, leading her on.

"Likely," Kate's face had gone pale. "Many of them are. It suits you. It is very pretty."

"I'm glad you like it," she said. "I wanted you to see it. You say you saw one like it?"

Kate Paxton appeared suddenly wary. "Probably close to it. They all resemble one another to a degree."

Gale pretended disappointment. "I thought you meant you'd seen the exact mate of it somewhere. I mean, by the way you spoke just now."

The former star's expression was veiled.

"I'm sorry. I didn't intend to give that impression."

"It seemed like an exciting coincidence," Gale went on.

Kate smiled coolly. "I'm sorry to let you down. But you really shouldn't worry. It is a very nice locket." Then she looked past Gale and with new warmth said, "Here is our author, Mr. Henderson."

Jack came up to stand by Gale's chair. "A long overdue author," he said with an air of apology. "Those sleeping pills really worked. Not only did I sleep all night I only woke up a little while ago."

Gale eyed his still bandaged head. "It probably did you good," she said. "How do you feel?"

"Much better," he said. "And you?"

"I've recovered," she smiled. "I missed you last evening."

"I'm sure I'd have missed you as well," Jack said genially, "except for the fact I was knocked completely out by those pills. I'll be careful of them in future." He took some stapled sheets from a folder and passed one set to Kate and the other to her. "New scene I've written. It's marked where the substitution is to be made."

Kate scanned the sheets quickly. "Goody!" she exclaimed. "I'm still in it and you've given me some extra lines."

"A tribute to talent," Jack said with a smile.

"Thank you!" Kate said with pleasure. "I'll take these to my cabin if you young people will excuse me." She gave them a smile and was on her way.

Jack watched her go and turned to Gale. "She knows how to make an exit," he said.

She nodded and in a dry tone said, "Yes. I think you helped her very neatly."

He sat in the chair Kate had just vacated with a surprised expression on his boyish face. "Just what does that mean?"

Then Gale quickly told him. About the cameo and how she had come by it and her plan to test the reactions of the various people who had seen it on her. She finished by saying, "I know Kate Paxton recognised it if the others didn't but for some reason she denied it at the last minute. I can't think why!"

Jack said, "Could she be your ghost?"

"Kate!" Gale's tone was incredulous.

"You said she acted suspicious about the cameo. It must mean something."

"Not that Kate is the one posing as Hedda's ghost. She's much too honest for that."

He looked wise. "But not too honest to

lie about the cameo."

She frowned thoughtfully. "That is something I can't understand," she admitted.

"I think the search for Joseph Holland has been abandoned," Jack said. "I talked with the Captain just now and he was very evasive."

"I'm not surprised," she admitted.

"I pointed out that I didn't inflict this blow on my own head," Jack said. "But he still didn't show any enthusiasm."

She sighed. "Then it is hardly the moment for me to impress him with stories of ghostly perfume and skeleton fingers placing a locket on my neck while I slept."

"I don't think you'd find him a sympathetic audience," was Jack's grim comment.

Gale looked at him wide-eyed. "What are we going to do, Jack?" She touched her fingers to the cameo. "This means whoever it is has access to my cabin at any time!"

"Not a pleasant thought when you know it could be the lunatic Joseph Holland," Jack said. He got up. "I'm on my way to have a talk with Mervin Hawley now. I'm going to ask his advice."

She got up as well. "He has plenty of problems of his own with the picture."

"This concerns him," Jack said. "If things go on this way it's more than likely he'll have to abandon the project."

Her eyes met Jack's. "I wonder if that is what is behind these happenings?"

"Could be. And then it might be something entirely different."

She walked as far as the end of the lounge with him. Then he went outside to look for Hawley while she walked down the dark corridor in the direction of her room. She had only gone a short way when a door opened behind her and she heard a voice softly call her name.

Surprised she stopped and turned to see Kate Paxton standing in the doorway of a cabin. She motioned to Gale and in a low voice said, "I want to speak to you."

Gale went back and entered the modest cabin. She said, "Yes?"

Kate had closed the door. Now she turned to her with a troubled expression on her once lovely face. She said, "I lied to you in the lounge a little while ago. I have seen that locket before. I recognised it at once." She paused. "Turn it and look at the back. You should find initials there. Small and in Old English script."

Gale gave her a quick glance and then examined the cameo as she had asked. Kate was right. The initials were there. She could read them plainly, "H.G."

Chapter Eight

"The last time I saw that locket Hedda Grant was wearing it," Kate said quietly.

Gale stared at her. "So this did belong to my aunt." A strange expression had come to the face of the older woman. "I saw it on Hedda's neck the night she vanished. She was wearing it when she left the party in the ballroom. I remember clearly. I mentioned it to her and told her how much I liked it."

"But if that was the case," Gale said slowly, "this locket should now be somewhere at the bottom of the ocean."

"One would expect so." The actress paused. "You say you found it among your things?"

Gale nodded quickly. Improvising, she said, "It was in my jewel box. I think my mother must have put it there before she died. I hadn't paid any attention to it since I knew nothing about its history." This at least seemed slightly more convincing than saying a phantom had slipped it on her throat in midnight darkness.

Kate Paxton looked somewhat sceptical. "Possibly Hedda may have put it away before whatever happened took place. It could be the locket was found with her belongings and sent to your mother as next of kin."

"That must have been it," Gale agreed a little too hurriedly.

The ageing actress offered a cynical smile. "Unless Hedda has come back from the dead to make you a present. I think we can accept she removed it before she went over the side to her death. It is interesting to see it again."

"I'm not sure I feel completely at ease wearing it," Gale admitted. "I'm sick of all this talk about Hedda. Her shadow seems to hang like a pall over the ship."

"I think Hawley was wrong to do this film," Kate said. "But it's too late to change that now."

Gale was facing the actress in the small cabin. "Why do you say that?"

Kate Paxton took a deep breath. She was wearing a chic black dress that gave her a regal air. She waved her to a chair. "Sit down a minute and I'll tell you." She glanced uneasily toward the cabin door. "It's difficult to talk when we meet outside. You can never tell who may overhear us."

"I know."

Kate sat on the bed facing her. "I think it was wrong for Mervin Hawley to stir this whole thing up again because I feel your aunt's death is unfinished business. Hawley should have let it be forgotten with the passing of this old ship."

"If you feel that way why did you agree to play a part in the film?"

The older woman shrugged. "Because Hawley pressed me. He was anxious to use as many people who had known Hedda as possible. Because he offered me twice my usual price these days and I needed a picture and the money." She paused and in a candid tone, "Because I thought there might be trouble and I'm too curious by nature to want to miss it."

Gale smiled ruefully. "You seem to have had plenty of reasons."

"Isn't that so?" Kate agreed.

"What sort of trouble did you expect?"

The former star gave her a searching glance. "You know the sort of woman Hedda was!"

"Not really. I've heard stories. Some of them oddly different. Judging by my mother's experience she was very difficult. She certainly wasn't any sort of sister to her and never had the slightest interest in me."

"That was true of Hedda in everything," Kate said. "She was a warped, jealous person. Her talent was exceptional but in the end her ego ruined her. No one wanted to hire her and she had become an alcoholic."

"Her husband was her agent. You'd think he would have tried to influence her."

"Jerry Hall?"

"Yes. He was her last husband, wasn't he?"

The other woman nodded. "Yes. She and Jerry had been married some years before she vanished. At first I think he did try. But when she betrayed him again and again he lost interest. Hollywood's favourite topic for a time was Hedda and her latest male conquests. Our good director was one of them."

Gale was surprised. "Mervin Hawley?"

"Yes. He'd been a leading man for a while. In those days he hadn't put on weight and his hair was a golden colour. He was really something! Hedda lost no time in adding him to her list of admirers."

"She was married to Jerry Hall then?"

"Of course. But Jerry wouldn't dare make any complaints. She'd sulk and rave and not show up on the set for days if he

did. By that time she had gained the reputation of being temperamental and some of
the big companies wouldn't hire her. Jerry
couldn't risk more scenes and losing the
ones that were still willing to take a chance
on her. So he allowed her to do as she
pleased."

"But he must have hated her!"

"I'm sure he did. You could see it in him
at the last. The affair with Hawley broke
up and Hedda moved on to a new interest
but I know for a fact Jerry Hall and
Hawley never spoke to each other from
that time on."

Gale frowned. "From what you tell me it
must have been Jerry Hall who killed her!
She had certainly done all she could to
drive him to it."

"True. But I don't believe it was Jerry
who pushed her overboard. In spite of all
that had happened he had loved her in the
beginning. And he was not a murderer by
type. He wasn't that sort at all. I met him
again shortly before he was killed in that
plane crash and I know he was genuinely
broken up by Hedda's death. He had been
drinking and he kept repeating what a pity
her death was and what a star she might
have been if things had been different."

"Yet you don't think she was a suicide."

There was a silence between them in the small cabin. Then Kate said, "No."

"So you must suspect someone?"

Kate's eyes met hers. "I do."

Gale felt she might be about to hear some important revelation. There was an air about the former star that suggested she knew something about the mystery. It might be some vital clue she had kept secret for years and was now about to divulge.

Gale asked, "Do you think it was Joseph Holland? That the mad artist is on board the *Britannia* now?"

Kate smiled knowingly. "Poor Joe Holland! He was another of Hedda's victims! He painted at least a half-dozen portraits of her at a time when his fee was tremendous and she didn't pay him a cent for them. She only complained they were second-rate. Joe was always a nervous, irritable little man. And yet when she vanished from the ship that night he was one of the hardest hit. He came to me with the news and there were tears in his eyes."

"What did he look like?"

"He was small, as I've said, had a pinched face and perhaps there was a little of the feminine in his manner. In his nature too. He loved gossip and fine clothes.

But that was thirty years ago. He's spent most of the years since in private asylums. He was rather nondescript in features. I doubt if I'd know him if I met him today."

"I suppose that is possible," Gale said.

The veteran actress smiled bitterly. "You'd be surprised if you knew how often it happens. The years change us. Time is the joker! The spoiler! We learn that soon in show business."

"If you rule out Holland as the killer you must suspect someone else. Could it be Mervin Hawley?"

"It could be," the actress admitted. "Hawley is a strong-willed person. Vehement in his hates. Yes, Hawley could have killed her if she'd taunted him enough." She spoke thoughtfully as if debating the possibility with herself.

"And that could be why he wanted to make this film?"

"I doubt it," Kate said. "If he had been guilty I think he would have been sensible enough to put it out of his mind afterward. He'd not want to come back to the scene of the crime and relive it all by making a film of the events."

"So you don't really suspect him?"

Kate shrugged. "I'd rather say I'd be surprised if it turned out to be him."

"But you do think the murderer is on the *Britannia*?"

She nodded. "Yes. And I think you are in danger because you are re-living the part of Hedda in the film. The murderer will want to stop you. There have been signs of this already."

Gale stared at her. "But you don't leave many other suspects. Steve Benson was on board. And he admits he knew Hedda. But he was young then. She would have been much older than him."

Kate gave her a knowing smile. "Older women can sometimes exert a strong influence on young men. Hedda had a special fascination for men half her age."

"But I don't see Steve as a killer type. He gives the appearance of strength but I don't think he really has much character."

"This happened thirty years ago. What he lacked in strength he might have had in impulsiveness and the arrogance of youth!"

Gale opened her eyes wide. "You're saying that Steve Benson is the one who killed my aunt?"

"I wouldn't want you to repeat it."

"But you do believe it."

Kate Paxton sighed. "Let us say I suspect him more than anyone else. That is why I wanted to talk to you. Warn you against being with him alone."

The ship rocked gently as a reminder there were still high winds. Gale sat in shocked silence. She was certain that Kate Paxton was sincere in what she'd just told her. That she really suspected the handsome Steve Benson of being her aunt's murderer. And it was quite possible she was right. Steve had mentioned knowing Hedda and being one of her crowd but he had not stressed that he had also been on the *Britannia* when she vanished.

Thinking back quickly Gale now saw that Steve had been involved in several suspicious incidents. Particularly the business at the pool. Both she and Jack had linked him with that but for another reason. They had assumed his motive was to try and secure the lead for the demanding Jane Fair when it might, instead, have been the insane act of someone with a long guilty conscience.

She told Kate, "Jack and I thought Steve knew more about what happened at the pool than he pretended. He could easily have been the one who struck Jack down and then tried to drown me."

"I've been thinking about that," Kate said. "That is why I had to speak to you frankly."

"I'm grateful."

The older woman looked worried. "But you must promise not to tell anyone of this conversation. You mustn't quote me or drag me into it in any way."

Gale was not too happy to hear this request made. She stood up. "It may be difficult," she said. "But I'll not say anything."

Kate got up as well to see her to the cabin door. "It may sound like a selfish and stupid request but I feel we are all in great danger as long as we're on this lonely old ship. Also I am not sure about Steve. There is another possibility. I will tell you more when I've had time to investigate and consider. Until then not a word."

"Very well," Gale said. She was at the door now. She turned as another thought came to her. "The maid in charge of my section was on the ship during the times when Hedda was a passenger."

"Oh?"

"She seems to be a great admirer of Hedda," Gale went on.

"Hedda always had a way of charming servants. She enjoyed making slaves of them. It was a trick of hers!" Kate Paxton's tone was coldly derisive.

Gale gave her a troubled look. "I suppose that fitted in with her nature," she said. "At any rate this maid, Maggie Dever, appears to have adored her. And she claims she found Jerry Hall with Hedda's maid in his arms on that last voyage."

Kate lifted her eyebrows. "I had never heard that Jerry's taste ran to maids. But it wouldn't surprise me. He had come to be a lonely and desperate man. He might have turned to anyone for companionship."

"It seemed to me that Hedda must have known about them as well if they were indiscreet enough to let the maid surprise them," Gale said.

"Perhaps she did."

"And that is why I've wondered if her husband murdered her because of that extra motive."

"I doubt it," Kate said.

"And I've wondered what happened to that maid. She seems to have vanished almost as completely as my aunt once she reached New York. No one ever heard of her again."

Kate Paxton made a weary gesture. "Girls like that! They come and go. She's probably happily married in the midwest somewhere and a grandmother by now."

Gale smiled faintly. "I suppose so. I just thought I should tell you."

"I'm glad you did," Kate said. But she didn't sound as if she was. In fact, her manner and tone had become strained all during the final part of the conversation and Gale began to feel she had stayed too long. She quickly said goodbye and went on to her own cabin.

Her thoughts were confused as she unlocked the cabin door and let herself in. And her state of mind wasn't cleared any by her discovery of Mervin Hawley standing there with his back to her as he studied her aunt's portrait. She uttered a surprised gasp. "How did you get in here?"

The big, florid-faced man turned to her with a smile. "I'm sorry to have upset you," he said. "I prevailed on Maggie to open the door for me. We've been cronies for years."

"I see," she said, slowly. Although she didn't. She couldn't imagine why Mervin Hawley would do such a thing. Surely it wasn't a crude overture. An attempt to force his attentions on her. She had never thought him the type for anything like that.

He gave a deep sigh. "I suppose you're wondering why I am here?"

"I suppose I am," she agreed in a thin voice.

"I wanted to talk to you a moment without attracting attention," he said.

She began to see a strangely striking parallel between this meeting and the one she had just had with Kate Paxton in her cabin. Kate had wanted to talk to her in private to explain some of her theories about the mystery of her aunt's long ago disappearance. Was Hawley about to do the same thing?

Mervin Hawley studied her solemnly. "Jack has just been talking to me. He's very upset about the many odd and violent happenings aboard. He doesn't consider the Captain is properly aware of the possible danger or likely to be. In short, he feels I am solely responsible for your safety."

"I think what happened at the pool has worried him a great deal," she said.

The big man nodded. "It has worried me as well. So have many other things. For instance, where did you get Hedda's locket?"

Her eyes opened wide. "You didn't say it was Hedda's locket before!"

"I do now."

"Why are you so sure?"

The director's face was grim. "Because I gave it to her. Jack told me some wild story about it being put on your neck while you were asleep."

She faced him defiantly. "It's no wild story. It's the truth!"

The smile on the director's florid face was not a pleasant one. He said, "I hope you'll forgive me if I'm sceptical. What are you trying to prove with this ghost stuff? Have you decided to go the publicity I dreamed up one better!"

She shook her head. "I told Jack the truth."

He stared at her in silence a moment. "It's quite a story. Though I'm sure you got the locket through your mother."

"If you want to think that."

The director didn't seem to know what to make of her staunch stand. He ran a hand over his bushy white hair. "It is my intention to do right by you, Miss Bond. And even if Jack hadn't pointed out my responsibility I would be well aware of it. I think that up to now I have been fair with you."

"I have no complaint," she declared, looking down.

"Thank you," he said, his voice not quite so cutting. "It's my belief there is a scheme under way, for what reason I don't know, to stop me from completing this film. I'm certain all these mysterious happenings have been instigated to that end. And particularly to break you down."

"Why me?"

"Because you are indispensable to my making a successful box-office film of your aunt's story," he said. "You give the mystery an added interest. And with Francois Mailet's make-up you are a dead ringer for Hedda. Watching you on the set yesterday sent chills up and down my spine."

"Perhaps the person responsible for her vanishing was watching and felt the same way," she suggested. "And that is why I've been attacked."

"No," he argued. "That is only what whoever it is wants to make you think. They're going to try and force you to believe in Hedda's ghost. Once they've convinced you her phantom walks the *Britannia*'s decks they have the battle won. You mustn't go along with such ideas."

"What do you suggest?" she asked meekly, seeing that he was distressed and not wanting to upset him more.

"You can start to fight them by refusing to think of Hedda as the pale ghost of someone who disappeared in the ocean years ago," he said, gesturing with his big hands in his earnest desire to convince her. "Think of her as the lovely woman and vital person she really was."

She gave him a knowing look. "I have heard all about her," she said. "From my mother and a lot of others."

"I know the sort of things you've heard," he declared harshly. "Just keep in mind that a great deal of it has to be merely vicious gossip! Hedda had her faults. In her later years she became jealous of your mother and she drank too much and gave the people for whom she worked a lot of trouble. But she was a great artist and don't let anyone tell you different. I knew her better than most people!"

"So I've heard."

The director's red face turned a shade of purple. "I don't know what you've heard and I don't care," he said. "Just so long as you think of Hedda as a living person and not a ghost!"

"But she was murdered! Perhaps in this cabin! And her body tossed overboard."

"No one can say for sure what happened beyond the fact she undoubtedly went into the sea," Mervin Hawley said. "She may have taken her own life. She wasn't happy at the time. I think the official verdict more or less hinted that."

Gale looked at him directly. "You were in love with her, weren't you?"

He hesitated. "All right. I'll admit that," he said after a minute. "It was over before that last voyage."

"But she was married at the time."

"To someone who didn't appreciate her. Who didn't hesitate to cheat on her." He gave Gale a worried look. "Some time ago I suggested you talk with Kate Paxton. I think I was wrong in that."

"Why?" she asked in surprise, mindful of her recent talk with the former star.

"Because Hedda's husband and Kate were very close. Kate thought she was in love with him. So you can hardly expect to get a fair picture of events from her."

It was another shattering bit of news. Gale stared at the earnest big man in shocked surprise. And all at once she realised her disadvantage in attempting to reconstruct the events of that shadowed night of thirty years ago on which her aunt had vanished. She knew so little of the people involved and the actual motives that had driven them. The gap of time stood between her and them and it was unlikely she would ever do better than hear the various sides of the story and come to her own conclusions.

Mervin Hawley spoke again, interrupting her thoughts. "Don't expose yourself to possible danger and come to me at once if anything unusual happens."

She was tempted to smile at this obtuse advice since he had received her story of the locket so badly. She said, "I intend to be careful."

He hesitated a moment longer. "One more thing."

"Yes?"

"I'd appreciate it if you wouldn't wear that cameo." Having delivered himself of this surprising statement he headed for the cabin door. He let himself out without another word.

Gale watched after him. He had given himself away in asking that she not wear the cameo. For some apparent reason it meant a great deal to him. The sight of it bothered him. By his own admission he had given it to Hedda Grant. And Hedda had been wearing it the very night of her death. If he had been dancing with her only a short time before she vanished he must have noticed it. Did it form a link in his memory with what had happened to her aunt, a link he'd prefer to forget?

After a moment Gale went into the bedroom and rang the bell for Maggie Dever, the maid. While she waited she carefully took off the cameo and placed it in her jewel box. She had just finished doing this when the maid entered the cabin.

"Yes, Miss?" the old woman smiled at her.

But Gale was stern. "When I returned just now I found Mr. Hawley in my cabin. He said you let him in."

An uneasy expression crossed Maggie's pale lined face. "I did, Miss. He said he wanted to wait for you and knowing you were good friends I thought there would be no harm done."

"But there was!" Gale said. "I was shocked to come back and find him making himself at home here."

"I'm sorry, Miss," the maid quavered.

"I do not want you to let anyone in here without my permission," Gale went on firmly. "Not anyone. Do you understand that?"

The maid nodded. "I do."

"I'll be very angry if it happens again," Gale promised. "I hope you understand that."

"I won't forget, Miss," Maggie Dever said contritely. "I'd never have done it if I'd known you might take offence."

"Well, you know now. And the rule applies to anyone."

Gale dismissed the maid feeling reasonably sure the old woman would be more careful in future. She had been doubly emphatic in her condemnation since she suspected that Maggie knew more about the midnight visitor and the scent of roses that had filled her cabin than she pretended to. And she felt in the same way the maid could offer some explanation about the cameo that had suddenly appeared around her throat. Maggie had pretended not to have seen it before but if all the others had noticed Hedda wearing it, wasn't it likely the maid who had taken such interest in the star would have been impressed by the locket?

After a few moments Gale decided she would take a leisurely bath before lunch. She hoped that it might relax her and rest her nerves. The bathroom was off the bedroom and neither of these rooms had any direct light but depended on electricity. The portholes were both in the living-room of the suite. Now she went into the bedroom and turned on the lights and on into the bathroom and switched the lights on in there. She ran the tub, put in some bath oil capsules and then slowly undressed.

She was hardly conscious of the continued mild heaving of the old liner as she settled back in the warm tub. It was really helpful and she congratulated herself for thinking of it. No amount of quick showers could offer her this feeling of comfort and ease. She closed her eyes and let her body soak in the warm water. She had no idea how much time passed, once the water seemed cooler and she turned on the hot water and filled the tub almost to the edge.

It was just as she was thinking of getting out and towelling herself and dressing for dinner that the lights in the bathroom suddenly blacked out with no warning. She sat in the tub staring up in the darkness of the steam-filled room and wondering what had happened. Quite often there had been a brief break in the electric current. The *Britannia*'s lighting plant was as old as the liner and Maggie had confided that it was being kept operating on this final voyage with the equivalent of hay wire and adhesive tape.

She decided to wait in the tub a moment and see if the lights came on soon. If it followed the previous precedent they would. And there was no advantage in hurrying from the tub since the bedroom would be in darkness and she couldn't dress and fix her hair in the faint light that leaked in from the living-room.

These were the thoughts running through her mind when she heard the creaking sound. As if the bathroom door was being ever so gently opened. It was distinct from the weary overall creaking and groaning of the vessel itself as she strained in the windy sea. This was close at hand. It could only be the door!

Someone was furtively entering the pitch-black bathroom.

As Gale cowered in the tub with growing fear her nostrils were suddenly filled with a familiar odour! The odour of roses!

Chapter Nine

And then before she could make a move or even collect her thoughts the terror was upon her. The odour of roses became overpowering and there was a rustling sound from the darkness close to her and at the same instant cold, cruel hands gripped her by the shoulders. She screamed and fought against her unknown attacker. And all too soon she realised what her assailant was attempting to do. With maniacal strength she was pressed down until she was barely able to keep her nostrils free of the bath water.

And she cried out her fear once more and scratched and clawed at the hands that held her in their intractable grip. She might as well have fought against stone or steel. It did no good! And now she was actually being forced down below the water. Somehow she held her breath and fought to free herself. But there was no relief! It seemed that at last her enemy had won! If this was the ghost of Hedda she would soon know the satisfaction of vengeance. Gale was sure she would drown in the tub.

It would be put down as an accident and add a macabre twist to the legend of the *Britannia*'s haunting by the famed star.

Sensing a momentary easing of one of the hands she managed to break away and lift her head above the water again. And once more she uttered a strangled call for help and pleaded for mercy. After a hectic moment she was again shoved harshly down below the surface of the water. She was weary now and knew she could battle no more. Her time had come to die. To die stupidly of drowning in a small bathtub with the ocean all around her. The irony of it!

And then the hands released her and even though the bathroom remained in darkness she knew she was all at once alone again. Her attacker had taken fright and run off for some reason. Weakly she grasped the edge of the tub and leaned her head against it.

From the bedroom she heard Maggie's frightened voice. "Miss Bond! Are you there?"

Mustering every ounce of her strength she called out weakly. "I'm in here. In the tub. I was taking a bath when the lights went out."

Maggie Dever came across the bedroom

to the bathroom door. "I can't think what's the matter, Miss," she said. "The lights are on everywhere else but in here. It must be a fuse. I'll have the steward check." She hesitated. "Are you all right?"

"Yes," Gale managed, feeling some better. She raised herself in the tub. "I'd rather you didn't leave me for a moment."

"Just as you say, Miss," the maid said. "If you want to dry yourself here is a towel."

"Thank you," Gale's voice was still thin from nerves. She got out of the tub and took the big proffered towel from Maggie. The maid held one end of it and helped to give her a brisk drying. When this was done the old woman fetched her dressing gown and she put it on and tied the sash. By now she was almost herself again.

She asked Maggie, "Did you notice the odour of rose perfume in the bathroom just now?"

"No, Miss," the old woman said blankly.

"And you didn't see anyone come out and go through the bedroom when you came in?" Gale wanted to know, a sharp note in her voice.

The old woman shook her head. "No, Miss."

They were standing in the bedroom now

188

and Gale could see the figure of the maid clearly even in the modest light coming in from the other room of the suite. She could just catch a glimpse of the expression on the pale lined face of Maggie Dever. And she was surprised to see no sign of guilt there.

She decided it would be pointless to tell her story to Maggie. The maid simply wouldn't believe it. So she said, "I was sure I heard someone moving about out here."

"It must have been me, Miss," the old woman said helpfully. "Now I'll go and see the steward about those fuses if you are all right."

"Go ahead," she told her in a resigned voice.

She stood for a long moment in the shadowed bedroom after Maggie had gone. It was unbelievable. Once again someone had deliberately tried to kill her and kill her in a way to make it seem like an accident. In spite of Mervin Hawley's harsh warning she found herself asking if those cruel hands that had once again tried to take her life were of this world? It seemed they must be the ghostly, avenging hands of the dead Hedda Grant!

Gale studied the dark corners of the bedroom with fear in her lovely eyes. If she had been visited by a living person it seemed almost certain that it had been with the collusion of Maggie Dever. Yet the maid had come to her rescue and when she'd questioned her just now she had given every appearance of being innocent. True, she had denied there had been any smell of roses and Gale knew the odour had been too strong to ignore. But what if the odour was of a phantom nature and evident to her nostrils alone?

The lights came on as quickly as they had gone out. And all the nightmare atmosphere seemed to vanish in the brilliant light. It was mid-day and there was no reason for her to feel afraid, no need for her to dwell on spectres. And then she remembered the horror she had endured in that dark bathroom only short minutes ago and she shivered.

She was almost dressed when Maggie Dever came back into the room. "It was the fuse, Miss," the old woman said brightly. "Hawkins replaced it and I see you have the lights again."

"Thank you," Gale said.

"Don't give it a thought, dear," Maggie said. "You go on to your lunch when you're ready and I'll clean up while you're gone." And with this the old woman went out.

Gale was at the dresser fixing her hair when the phone rang. The unexpected sound made her jump and she realised in what a state her nerves were. She got up and answered the phone. It was Jack.

"What's keeping you?" he wanted to know. "I'm calling from the dining room. I've been waiting here for you to join me at lunch as you promised."

"A slight delay," she said meaningly.

There was a startled pause at the other end of the line. Then Jack asked sharply, "Anything wrong?"

"Not now."

"You're talking in riddles!"

"At the moment everything is a riddle. I'm almost dressed."

"How long will you be?"

"Just the time it takes to do my hair," she said. "Why don't you meet me here at the cabin?"

Jack sounded thoroughly disturbed. "Would it be best?"

"I think so."

"I'm on my way," he promised.

She put down the phone and was about to go back to the dresser and finish her hair when for the first time since the lights had come on she glanced in the bathroom door. And what she saw made her halt with

191

a pounding heart. Then she moved slowly across to the door with an awed expression on her lovely face. For there on the tiles was a long strip of seaweed similar to the type she had found in the room before. It seemed her caller had indeed come from afar! From beneath those green watery depths of her nightmare!

Stunned by her discovery she went back to the dresser and tried to again concentrate on making her hair presentable. A moment later she heard Jack's knock on the door and went to let him in.

The first thing he did was take her in his arms with a smile and give her a long, comforting kiss. Then he looked at her and with his arms still around her said, "I needed that. And you looked far too lovely to ignore."

She said, "It's happened again, Jack."

His boyish face shadowed as he let her go. "What?"

She told him. And then she led him to the bathroom door. Pointing to the seaweed she asked him, "What do you make of that?"

He studied it grimly. "Someone has a wonderful sense of the dramatic," he said. "It's too expertly staged to be anything more than a trick to frighten you."

Gale looked up at him. "I am terrified!"

"That's how they mean to keep you," Jack said grimly. "It's obviously their plan to work on your nerves until you're not able to work. Then Hawley will be forced to abandon the picture after wasting a fortune leasing this old ship."

"You make it sound as if someone was out to get at him."

"He will be the chief financial sufferer if the film isn't made," Jack told her. "All the rest of us will have to be paid along with the costs for the ship."

She frowned slightly. "But I see it differently. I think whoever it is must be insane and trying to murder me because I'm playing Hedda's role."

"We're back to Joseph Holland again!"

"Hardly anyone seems to think it could be that little man even if he has managed to get on board some way," Gale told him seriously.

Jack was quick to ask. "Then who do they think it is?"

"I've heard so many theories. I'm completely muddled."

"So is every one else, including the Captain," he said. "We'd better get on to the dining salon. We've barely time left for lunch. Hawley is planning to do a scene in the ballroom this afternoon."

She showed surprise. "He didn't seem to think it was smooth enough when he was here."

"The ocean has quieted a lot in the last hour," Jack said. And with a significant glance, "But then I suppose you've hardly been in a position to notice."

"That's so true," she said as they left the cabin.

They hurried through lunch and then joined the others in the main ballroom where Mervin Hawley had set up his cameras on one side of the big room so he could use the full ballroom and orchestra stand along with a portion of the table section in the scenes he was about to do.

Along with the battery of cameras and strong floodlights there was the usual confusion as the technicians got the set ready. Sound men tested hidden microphones and as usual Hawley was everything at once guiding the operation. Gale admired him for his attention to detail. He took nothing for granted and while he frequently consulted with his assistants he plainly did not depend on them.

The orchestra assembled as they would be playing background music all through the sequence. This necessitated special instructions for them and a lot of extra work on the sound details. While the director coped with this new problem Gale took her regular chair next to Kate Paxton.

The actress was already made up and in the costume she wore when she made her single appearance to go to one of the tables and inform Gale, in the role of Hedda, that she was wanted by someone on the phone in her cabin. It was a long distance call and urgent, Kate would announce. Actually it was a plot device of Jack's to get the soon-to-be-murdered girl alone in her cabin.

She said, "Francois is in the nearest cabin on the left. Costumes are in the room opposite. Better hurry. They'll soon be wanting you."

"You can tell them where I've gone," Gale said and hurried out to the cabin.

She found Francois waiting for her and in a strangely quiet mood. He barely spoke to her and didn't seem to want to talk at all. Finally when he had finished with her, he said, "I've been thinking about that cameo you had on this morning. It was an interesting piece and it suited you."

Gale smiled her surprise. "You wouldn't tell me that then."

"I hadn't decided about it," Francois snapped and turned his back on her as a signal of dismissal. She left thinking what an odd little man he was.

Her costume for this scene was an elaborate evening dress of the period covered with glistening spangles of the same shade. It was a dazzling outfit and took careful fitting. The elderly wardrobe mistress fussed and worried until she thought that every detail was right. Then she stepped back with a smile on her fat, matronly face.

"It is good now," she said with the trace of a Teutonic accent.

"A truly wonderful gown," Gale agreed, studying herself in the long three-sided mirror. She had just finished admiring the dress when the door of the cabin was flung open and star Jane Fair came striding in.

The brunette star was wearing an orange dress with low bodice and slim shoulder straps. Gale saw at once that one of the shoulder straps had broken and Jane was holding it in place. With an angry glance at the wardrobe mistress she announced in her throaty voice, "This dreadful costume is coming apart!"

"I'll fix it!" The wardrobe woman promised and dived for a needle and thread.

Jane Fair took a seat in one of the several plain chairs. With a scathing glance in Gale's direction she said, "Well, they didn't spare any expense on your dress! That's easy to see!"

"Yours is very attractive," Gale told her. This was the first actual time they had exchanged words off the set and she felt she should try to hold some sort of polite conversation with the irate star for the good of the company.

Jane Fair showed disgust. In her throaty voice she exclaimed, "This is a rag Mervin has given me. So I'll just cost him a little money. They're having to hold everything up until this is repaired. So you needn't hurry."

"It's only minor, thank goodness," Gale said, wishing she could leave but sure the star would be even more annoyed if she did.

"That may be your opinion, it certainly isn't mine," Jane Fair said coldly. And to the wardrobe mistress she warned, "Be careful to sew that strap at exactly the right angle or I'll rip it off again!"

"Yes, Miss," the wardrobe woman was plainly in an abject state as she went about trying to repair the torn strap.

Jane Fair now stared at Gale. "You do somehow look different in your make-up," she said. "Francois is a marvel. He gives your face intelligence. Steve swears you're so like Hedda Grant you make his flesh creep."

Gale had been annoyed by the first part of the star's comments. But the second half intrigued her. It fitted in so well with the suspicions that had been growing since her talk with Kate Paxton. Her feeling that Steve was the one she had to fear.

She said, "Why should my resembling my aunt make his flesh creep?"

Jane Fair looked bored. "It seems Steve and Hedda were very good friends. Although I must confess I should have expected better taste in a star like Hedda Grant, Steve can be so utterly common."

"I had no idea he and Hedda were really close," she said.

"He claims he may have been the last person to see her alive," Jane Fair went on in her throaty way. "But then you know how he goes on. Anything to make himself important. I really don't know how Mervin puts up with him."

Gale tried to hide her distaste for the unpleasant Jane since she felt the conversation might pay dividends. Casually, she told her, "I think he wanted to hire as many people as he could who knew my aunt or were in some way associated with her."

A malicious gleam showed in the brunette's eyes. "Of course I was a tot in the cradle when it all happened so it doesn't apply to me. Hawley hired me for my talent alone. It shows you how old Steve must be when you consider he was around in the business that long ago." She paused and smiled cattily. "And of course you were hired to build up the sensation because you are her niece. So you needn't really worry about your acting, need you? It isn't all that important." The wardrobe woman had finished with the strap and stepped back with a worried look to await Jane's opinion of her work. The star stood before the mirrors and murmured, "It will do."

Gale and the arrogant Jane Fair returned to the ballroom together and Gale's cheeks burned as she realised all eyes in the big room were focused on them. She knew that Jane must have created a good big scene about her dress when she'd left the set in a rage and it was widely known she and the brunette avoided each other except when they were before the cameras so this double entrance would add to the sensation.

She caught Steve Benson gazing at them from the corner of her eye and thought he looked decidedly uneasy. Jane Fair went across to the middle of the ballroom floor where Mervin Hawley was standing talking to the assistant director.

"I'm ready to work again, Mervin," she said in her queenly way.

The big man's florid face showed annoyance. "That's good news." And he looked around. "What about Miss Bond?"

Gale stepped forward so he could see her and smiled. "Ready," she said.

The director brightened. "Great. The dress is fine and the total effect is just what I've been wanting. We'll start the scene at once."

And they did. It began with a group at the table. The actor playing the role of the ship's Chief Officer excused himself first. Then Gale danced with Steve Benson and they carried on a small argument about her flirting with the officer. Then they went back to the table and Steve invited Jane Fair, in the role of the other woman, to dance. While these two were dancing Kate Paxton entered as the maid and informed Gale of the long distance call waiting her in her cabin. The scene ended with Gale leaving the ballroom and Steve hurriedly excusing himself from an annoyed Jane Fair and following. This was a complete sequence in the fictional version of Hedda Grant's life story. As usual Hawley wasn't satisfied with the first run through. He insisted that they do it all again.

Then he concentrated on tiny segments of the scene and had the cameras move in for more intimate angles. Before the session of shooting ended it was after five-thirty.

Everyone seemed pleased with what had been accomplished. The general opinion appeared to be that it had been the best day's work since they had begun the strange voyage to film the mystery. Gale knew she was dreadfully tired and after she had quickly slipped out of the elegant gown started down the corridor to her cabin. She wanted to rest a little before Jack picked her up for dinner at seven.

Actress Kate Paxton joined her. "I see you've made a new friend," she said.

Gale glanced at her with bitter amusement. "Jane! I had to talk to her. We met in the dressing room."

Kate rolled her eyes. "You should have been on the set when the strap burst off her dress. She gave a showing of dramatics that would have shamed Bernhardt!"

"I can imagine," she said. "But maybe it was good we met in there after all. She said something about Steve that made me think your theory about him may be right."

The ageing actress gave her a blank look. "My theory about him?"

"You know what I mean," Gale insisted, slightly flustered.

They had come to the door of Kate's cabin and she halted. With no hint of expression, she said, "I'm afraid I don't."

"You know! The private talk we had!"

"Oh, a private talk!" Kate Paxton stressed the word private. "I'm afraid I don't recall anything that was said." She smiled thinly. "But then that isn't important since it was just a private talk, wasn't it?"

"Yes," Gale said. "I'm sorry." Kate Paxton merely nodded and went into her cabin and closed the door.

Gale continued on to her own cabin knowing she had annoyed the older woman by referring to their earlier talk. It was clear Kate was going to strictly enforce her rule that no mention of the discussion was to be made. Gale had not felt it any harm to speak of it to each other. But Kate felt differently and so she must be careful to go along with her wishes in future. Perhaps it was best.

As soon as she reached her own cabin

she went into the bedroom and stretched out on the bed. She fell asleep almost at once. And when she awakened the room was almost completely dark. As she gradually became more alert she suddenly realised she was not alone. Someone was moving about in the shadows of the bedroom. She sat up with a scream!

Then from the shadows came a familiar voice. "It's just me, Miss Bond!" It was Maggie Dever speaking. "I'm sorry I frightened you. I saw you were still sleeping and I was going out to come back later and do the bed."

"You gave me a bad scare," Gale told her.

"I didn't mean to, Miss Bond. You know my habit of going about this suite in the darkness. I suppose one of these days it will get me in trouble."

"I should think so," was Gale's answer as she swung her legs off the bed. "There are plenty of things to stumble on and a broken bone at your age is not a joke."

"And that's the truth, Miss," the old woman said as she switched on the overhead lights.

Gale's eyes were dazzled for a moment. She looked at the veteran maid and said, "I thought I saw you watching us work this afternoon."

"Indeed I was there," Maggie Dever said happily. "It was wonderful with the music and dancing and all. Half of the stewards' staff was there to see it. And you looking so much like dear Hedda Grant!"

Gale smiled as she stood up. "I'm glad you enjoyed it." And then she had a sudden thought. "Did you recognise Steve Benson? He's the one playing my husband in the picture."

"Oh, yes! Everyone knows Mr. Benson. He's a popular star."

"I mean, did you recognise him from the old days. I hear he's been on the *Britannia* before. In fact, I understand he was a passenger on the voyage on which my aunt vanished. He was young then. But I believe he was friendly with her."

The old woman screwed up her face in concentrated thought. "Now let me see," she mused. "He would be much younger then as you say. I'm fairly sure I remember all them that was friendly with Miss Hedda."

"He wouldn't be much more than twenty-one or two at that time," Gale said.

"And his hair was two or three shades lighter," Maggie said, appearing to remember. "And he was a good deal thinner. Not that he's stout now but he has sort of filled out if you know what I mean."

"Then you do remember him?" Gale said, pleased.

"Indeed I do," Maggie went on eagerly now. "I didn't connect him with Steve Benson. But I see it was him now. Miss Hedda called him her moody boy and she used to tease him wicked. He was always sort of mooning around but Miss Hedda just poked fun at him."

"She wasn't seriously interested in him then?"

"No!" the old woman said with a laugh. "Many a time she had me send him away with the word she was somewhere on deck and she would be right here in her cabin."

"I knew you'd probably remember," Gale said pleased with her findings.

It wasn't until she sat down beside Steve, meticulously dressed in his dinner jacket and black tie as usual, that she had a chance to bait him with the information she'd gotten from the old woman.

She told him, "Someone was watching you on the set this afternoon who can remember you in the old days. She saw you on the trip you made with Hedda. The one that turned out to be Hedda's last crossing."

He looked worried. "Is that so?" he asked quietly.

"Yes. She says Hedda used to call you her moody boy."

Steve frowned. "Who told you all this stuff?"

"Isn't it true?" she asked innocently. "I understand you and my aunt were close friends."

The handsome leading man regarded her warily. "I knew her well enough."

Gale was impressed by his discomfiture. More and more she was coming to the conclusion he was the one to be watched. She said, "Then Maggie was right."

"Maggie?" he asked sharply. "Maggie who?"

"My maid," she said. "Maggie Dever. She's worked on this ship from the time it first went into service."

"I see," he said glumly, giving his attention to his food again.

"She remembers all about you and Hedda on that last voyage," Gale went on deliberately. "She has a wonderful memory for an old woman."

"So it seems," Steve said dryly. And then he changed the subject talking to her about the day's shooting and telling her how much he enjoyed her work. Jane Fair overheard this from across the table and shot them a look of daggers. At her side Jack sat quiet and plainly amused.

It was the Captain who caught all their attention next by saying calmly, "We've found clues to suggest the New York authorities may be right." He spoke in his quiet manner. "It looks as if we do have a stowaway. We've found a topcoat and black felt hat in one of the abandoned areas below. I wired New York."

Mervin Hawley was very interested. "Have you had a reply?"

"Yes," Captain Redmore said. "The hat and coat meet the description of those Joseph Holland had on when he escaped."

The director said, "Then he has to be on board!" His excitement showed in his strong face and Gale could picture him thinking up ways to exploit this situation and make the film even more sensational.

"No," the Captain disagreed. "I wouldn't say that."

"You mean?" Hawley said.

"I mean he could have gone over the side as Miss Hedda Grant did," Captain Redmore told him. "Holland was insane and he could easily have decided to end his life while in a depressed mood."

Hawley looked chagrined. "I hadn't thought of that," he admitted.

After dinner she and Jack went to the

main ballroom and danced for awhile. They left about ten and went for a stroll along the open deck before turning in for the night. The wind had died down and a big new moon shone down on a placid silver ocean. From a distance away they were able to spot the brilliant lights of another great liner as it passed them on its way back to New York. It was one of the more pleasant nights since they had been at sea.

Leaning with her at the rail Jack asked, "Make any progress with Steve?"

"Some," she said. "I baited him and he seemed upset to think that Maggie had remembered him."

"He and Jane weren't in dancing tonight," Jack said with a smile. "Maybe you gave him a headache."

"If he is to blame for any or all of what has happened I sincerely hope so," she said.

They went on the corridor and Jack kissed her good-night at the door of her cabin. As soon as he left her she experienced all the uneasiness she had known on other nights. And although she knew it was wrong to be so dependent on him she had to face the fact that she was always under the pressure of fear when she was by herself.

She let herself in and turned on the living-room lights. At first she didn't notice the shape on the floor. And when she did she couldn't move or speak for a second of frozen terror. Then she began to scream over and over again. For Maggie Dever was there on the floor by the fireplace in a motionless, crumpled heap!

Chapter Ten

A distraught Gale rushed to the cabin door and flinging it open shouted down the corridor for help. She remained at the door repeating her frightened cries until a middle-aged man in steward's uniform came hurrying to answer her calls for help. His plain face showed concern as he reached her.

"What is it, Miss?" he asked anxiously.

She pointed. "In there!"

The steward rushed into the cabin and as soon as he saw the figure on the floor came to a startled halt. He exclaimed, "Maggie!" And then with a glance at Gale who had followed him into the living-room of the cabin he went on over and knelt beside the fallen woman. He got up almost immediately and turned to her.

"I'll get the nurse," he said, starting for the door.

She was on the point of hysteria. "Don't leave me!" she begged.

The steward stood there hesitating for a moment. Then he said, "I can call for the nurse then." And he hurried across to the phone and made the call. After he'd given his message in urgent tones he put the phone down and announced, "She'll be here in a few minutes. And I've asked that the Captain be informed."

Gale kept her eyes averted from the body on the floor. "Can you tell what's happened?"

The steward's face was grave. "She's had a bad fall. Struck her head on one of the points of the fireplace railing." He paused. "I think she's done."

"Oh, no!" It was a genuine protest of sorrow on Gale's part. She had become very fond of the old woman.

The steward glanced at the motionless body. "I can't see how it could happen unless she was taken with a weak spell."

"She had a habit of coming in here in the dark and doing small routine things without bothering to turn on the lights," Gale remembered. "I warned her she might stumble over something."

The steward nodded and scanning the area near where Maggie lay said, "She might have been tripped by that footstool. It's just by her."

There was no time for further speculations as the nurse arrived along with Captain Redmore and one of the other ship's officers. It took only a moment for the nurse to pronounce the veteran maid dead. With a grim expression on his lined face the Captain gave instructions for the body's removal. There was another short interval before bearers came with a stretcher. The steward remained to clean up and at Captain Redmore's suggestion Gale accompanied him to his own quarters.

The living-room of the Captain's quarters was as luxurious as any of the best passenger cabins. It was located forward on A Deck and Gale had not been there before. She was too stunned to say much on the short walk to it and only after the Captain had seated her by his broad walnut desk and seen that she had a stiff glass of whisky did she begin to feel anything like normal.

Meanwhile the little man in his gold-braided uniform paced up and down before her, one hand behind his back, his own drink in the other. He said, "I'm not going to have you stay in that cabin."

"It hasn't been very lucky for me," she admitted. "And after what happened there tonight I don't think I'd ever be happy there again."

Captain Redmore nodded. "I can well understand that. Mr. Hawley wanted you to have this suite your aunt occupied chiefly for publicity purposes. Since the need for that is over I see no reason why you should not be transferred to a similar type suite in another section of A deck."

Gale looked up at the stern little man who controlled the destiny of the *Britannia* on this last voyage. "You do think what happened to Maggie was an accident?"

The Captain paused in his pacing to take a sip from his glass and then fix her with a stern expression. "What reason could there be to think otherwise? Who would want to harm her?"

Ever since the discovery of Maggie's body she had been overwhelmed with a feeling of guilt. She couldn't forget that she had deliberately taunted Steve Benson with quotes of what the veteran maid had said to her about him. She recalled Steve's uneasy reaction and knowing the suspicions concerning him she felt she might have been responsible for forcing him to murder the old woman.

Certainly she was now silenced for ever.

But all this was based on such assorted scraps of information and wild conjecture she hesitated to reveal her thoughts to the Captain. She felt he would certainly ask for some solid proof for her suspecting Steve of murder and she had none to offer. She saw that she had best keep silent until she at least had time to discuss this with Jack and ask his advice.

The Captain was staring at her. He repeated, "What reason would anyone have to harm poor old Maggie?"

She made a frustrated little gesture with her right hand. "I can't imagine! But some very strange things have been happening on this ship."

"I can agree with you there," Captain Redmore said grimly.

"It was an accident," Gale went on. "At least the nurse seemed certain of it."

"The cause of death was the point of one of those railing spikes penetrating the skull," he said. "If she stumbled in the darkness on that hardwood floor and hit it with her full weight I don't think there's any doubt the injury would have to be fatal. As it was."

"There were no other signs of violence?"

"None."

Gale was still worried. Still having doubts and feeling guilty. So she hazarded, "No indication that she might have been seized by someone and thrown down on the railing?"

The Captain stared at her. "Not that I know of. Why do you make such a suggestion?"

Gale looked down at her empty glass. "I don't know. I guess that after what happened at the pool my mind runs to violence."

"That was undoubtedly the work of Joseph Holland," the Captain said. "We've found some of his outer clothing. He's undoubtedly still in hiding somewhere aboard. But I can't see him murdering Maggie and I can't accept what happened as anything but an accident."

"Probably you are right," she agreed with some reservation in her tone.

There was a knock on the door of the Captain's cabin and he called out for whoever it might be to come in. The door opened and a troubled-looking Mervin Hawley stepped inside.

He came directly over to her. "What's this I hear about there being a death in your cabin?"

"Maggie Dever. She fell and died as a result," Gale said.

The director looked astonished and regretful. "Poor old Maggie! We had a long talk only today!"

"I remember," she said. And the director's florid face took on a deeper shade of red. It was evident he did as well. He had used his influence with Maggie to enter her suite without permission. Now he looked ashamed of his actions.

He turned to the Captain. "Well, at least there was no suspicious circumstances about her death."

Captain Redmore was standing behind his desk. "I think we may safely say that. But it is a most unhappy business. I have decided it would be best to move Miss Bond to another suite."

Mervin Hawley at once looked annoyed. "But why?"

"Surely it needs no explanation," the Captain said patiently. "I am sure Miss Bond would rest better in different surroundings after what has happened."

"But her being in the suite Hedda occupied is part of the production plan," the big man argued. "The press made a lot of it."

The Captain regarded him calmly. "Surely that phase of things is over with the picture well on its way?"

Hawley frowned. "I suppose so."

"So we'll move Miss Bond at once."

The director took the news with no sign

of enthusiasm. He glanced at her, and said, "Do you feel strongly enough about this to go to the trouble of changing your suite?"

She had many more reasons than Maggie's accident and death to cause her to quickly reply, "Yes. I would like to move."

The director hesitated and then turned to the Captain. "I guess that settles it," he said heavily.

Gale was baffled at his obvious disappointment. He surely could have no logical reason for wanting her to remain in the suite. Unless they were underhand reasons of which she knew nothing. It was a possibility. Hawley must still be regarded as one of those who might have had complicity in her aunt's death.

The Captain was as good as his word. He enlisted the services of two stewards and a maid and went along with Gale to supervise the transfer to a suite on the opposite side of the ship but leading from the same corridor. Not until she was safely installed in her pleasant new quarters did he offer her a polite goodnight. When he had gone she took a close look at the three-room suite. Its living-room had a motif of white and gold and was somewhat smaller than the other one. The bedroom was in rose and she observed with a wry glance the maid had carefully installed the smiling portrait of Hedda Grant on the dresser in exactly the same position it had occupied in the other room. At least she was to have this reminder of cabin A20. The bathroom was the same size and in the same location.

She had just finished her tour of inspection when there was a soft knock on her door.

Approaching it she asked cautiously, "Who is it?"

"Jack," was the answer that at once put her at ease. She let him in.

The red-haired young man's boyish face showed concern. "I just heard the news. I'm glad the Captain moved you."

She had closed the door and come back to stand near him. "Mervin Hawley almost stopped it."

He frowned. "Why?"

"I can't guess. He's a person with strong ideas."

"But surely he'd know how you must feel after what happened to Maggie in there?"

"I don't think our director is a terribly sensitive man," she said dryly. "Then again he may have had his own reasons for wanting me to stay there."

Jack glanced at her sharply. "Could be. What do you make of this accident?"

"I wish I could decide."

"What?"

"That it was an accident," she said with a sigh. "You know how I baited Steve Benson about Maggie tonight at dinner."

He nodded worriedly. "I've been thinking about that. Did you say anything to the Captain?"

"No. I'm sure he'd say I was imagining things again."

Jack's eyes met hers. "It begins to look as if Benson is the killer."

"If he is I'm sure he'll give himself away before the picture is finished."

"I don't know," Jack worried. "He might just sort of recede in the woodwork now and that will be the end of it all. If he did murder your aunt he's kept his neck safe for thirty years. He probably felt he had to silence Maggie to continue to protect himself. But I don't see him seeking out new victims."

"I don't agree," Gale said quietly. "I'm sure he'll try to get at me."

"He can't be that insane!"

"Not only because I'm constantly a reminder of Hedda while I play her role but because now he doesn't know how much

Maggie revealed to me."

Jack's brow wrinkled. "You make it sound very convincing."

"It's the way I see it," she said.

"But all this is assuming Steve Benson is the killer," Jack said, his face brightening a trifle. "And we're not by any means certain that he is."

"No. We're not," she had to agree.

"Even though Kate Paxton seems to suspect him she's given you no sound evidence of his guilt," Jack argued on. "And didn't she hint there was another person about whom she hadn't made up her mind."

"She did say something like that," Gale agreed. "But she's very frightened. When I discussed it with her today she pretended she'd never mentioned the subject."

"Careful lady!" he said grimly.

"Perhaps she's wise," Gale said. "The Captain seems positive Joseph Holland is hiding somewhere on the *Britannia*."

Jack touched the Band-Aid still on his temple. "I have a souvenir to prove that unless it was Steve who went amok down there." He glanced around the room. "In any case I'll feel better knowing you're here."

She smiled. "So will I."

He kissed her goodnight and left. For the first time in many nights Gale was able to go to sleep almost immediately. And as if to herald the beginning of better times ahead the next morning was sunny and warm. The company resumed their filming on deck and the picture went ahead much more quickly than before. Even the arrogant Jane Fair behaved a little more like a human being. But one thing both Jack and Gale noticed was how aloof Steve Benson had suddenly become. He said little to Gale and avoided her company whenever he could. This along with the absence of Maggie's frail little presence on the sidelines as they filmed the various scenes were the chief differences of which Gale was aware.

Another thorough search of the ship had not turned up the fugitive madman, Joseph Holland. But although Captain Redmore had seemingly given up worrying about the little man whom everyone felt was hidden somewhere aboard there were rumours of midnight raids on the galleys and food being filched.

Yet as one sunny day followed another and the weather continued warm the *Britannia* came to seem less like a ghost ship. Both company and crew were in a carefree relaxed mood and as the time of the old vessel's final cruise came close to an end it could almost be said she was no longer shadowed by the ghostly legend of the vanished Hedda Grant.

Gale had become much less apprehensive and often took long walks alone on deck both in the daytime and the evening. With her transfer from cabin A20 the whole atmosphere aboard the venerable liner seemed to have changed for the better. Only Mervin Hawley seemed to be growing increasingly moody and irritable as the picture neared its end. Perhaps it was because he had been working almost night and day and she also felt it was his perfectionist side bothering him again.

Jack went on deck with her after dinner one pleasant evening about ten days later and as they leaned against the railing, confided the trouble he was having with the famous director.

"Hawley is insisting on script changes," he said. "Now he's asking for a new ending."

Gale's eyebrows raised. "But we've already done the ending. The scene where the Chief Officer is cornered on the upper deck and confesses to killing Hedda."

"I know it," Jack said glumly. "Don't

think I haven't reminded him. But he's still determined to do another ending. Says the one we settled for wasn't realistic enough."

"Have you written the new one yet?"

"Not completely. I've only just gotten his suggestions." He gave her a knowing glance. "Now he wants Hedda's husband to be the guilty one."

Gale looked startled. "That means Steve will be playing the murderer. I wonder how he'll like that."

"Hawley hasn't told him yet."

She gave the young writer a knowing look. "Do you think it's a macabre joke on Hawley's part to make Steve Benson live fictionally a role he may have played in real life years ago."

There was a short silence between them. Jack stared out at the placid sea. "I don't think it's any joke on Hawley's part. But it could be a deliberately malicious gesture because he thinks Steve was Hedda's murderer and he wants to make him suffer through the crime again."

She said, "What do you think will happen?"

"I don't know. Whether he's guilty or not Steve is bound to raise a row about having his pleasant supporting role suddenly turned into that of a killer. It could hurt him for future pictures. Audiences tend to always identify actors who play villains in the same roles."

"Hawley knows that."

"And he's still determined to go ahead with this other ending," Jack said. "He must have strong reasons."

"And there isn't much time left," she pointed out. "Even if the weather holds. He only has the ship leased for the balance of this week."

"I've reminded him of that as well," Jack told her. "And he said he has the option to keep it for extra days. After all her only destination is the graveyard after this trip is over."

Later, Gale always marked the change in their mood and fortunes, with this casual discussion with Jack. After the warm day and evening the fog settled in around midnight. She was first aware of it when the old vessel began giving off hoarse blasts on her foghorn at regular intervals. This continued all night and into the morning. When she went on deck after breakfast the mist was so thick you could barely see a few feet ahead.

Once again spirits dropped and suspicions took over. Work was impossible. And as the fog remained the old vessel came to a standstill trapped in the ghostly mist and intermittently giving off her grim warning signal. Once again the phantoms closed in with a vengeance.

It was appropriate that at this time the storm should break out between director Hawley and his leading man. Jack had told Gale he'd turned over the new manuscript to Hawley. But she was not aware of Steve Benson's reaction until she met the classic profile on deck the third morning they were fogbound. She was not surprised to find him enraged, all their nerves were on edge from the constant inactivity, the phantom atmosphere of the nearly deserted old liner, and the bleating of the foghorn. In addition to this he had this special problem of the script change.

He was wearing a trenchcoat, his shoulders hunched dejectedly and a haggard expression on his weary, handsome face. Halting her on the lonely, fog-ridden deck he demanded, "Have you heard the latest news about the different ending?"

"I heard there was to be one."

"I refuse to do it!" Steve exclaimed angrily. "Hawley is using this sly trick to wreck my career. If I play this part as he wants I'll never be able to get anything but villain roles from now on."

She tried to sympathise. "I don't think that's true today. Actors play all sorts of parts."

He wasn't to be consoled. "I know! This whole production has been a farce from the start! The picture could have been made in Hollywood using long shots of the ship for realism. Bringing us all here? We're liable to wind up under the Atlantic with Hedda!"

"Why do you say that?" she stared at him.

"We're in serious danger in this fog," he raged. "And this is one of the most active lanes for shipping. It was here off the coast of Cape Cod the *Andrea Doria* was rammed. What chance do you think we'd have if one of those modern new liners should bear down on us?"

"It's not likely to happen."

"It has happened before," he reminded her grimly and thrusting his hands in the pockets of his trenchcoat he walked on to vanish in the mist. Gale stared after him, knowing he was badly upset and once again wondering how much he had been involved in her aunt's disappearance those long years ago. And whether he was the one she should fear now?

In the interlude of warm pleasant days she had not given it much thought. But now with the return of bad weather and the hostility among the company that had come with it she was bound to think of these things. Hawley had been taking an increasing amount of Jack's time and so she had not been able to discuss the situation with him as much as usual.

Braving the blasts of the foghorn she moved from A Deck to the one above it. It had been a favourite strolling place with her since the time she had first met Jack up there. She had grown very fond of the young writer and she was fairly sure that he returned her feelings. It seemed likely they would go on seeing each other after the picture and last cruise of the *Britannia* was over. And she was certain they would always think of the old liner, occasionally with feelings of remembered fear, but she hoped, more often with affection as the place where they had first grown to know one another.

The creaking of the liner's ancient plates mingled with the blasts from her foghorn to produce an atmosphere of supreme melancholy. But at least the sea was calm, Gale thought, as she leaned over the rail. Not that she could catch a glimpse of it in this pea-soup fog. She could barely see the lifeboat near her as it swayed gently from its davits.

She had been there for some minutes when she glanced down the deck and saw the wraith-like figure coming out of the mist towards her. Because she was so alone up there and because she could not clearly discern the outlines of the figure she felt a sudden fear and held her breath for a second.

Then the phantom of the fog drew closer and she clutched the rail in sheer terror for she saw the woman approaching her wore a pillbox hat, a veil and long old-fashioned coat!

Once again her frightened eyes told her this must be the ghost of Hedda Grant. She had an impulse to turn and race down the slippery, wet deck in search of safety from this spectre risen from the murky ocean depths. But as panic closed in on her the phantom spoke and her voice was familiar.

"Is that you, Gale?" It was Kate Paxton who called to her.

With a wondrous feeling of relief Gale drew an easy breath again. All her fears had been for nothing. She had allowed the spooky atmosphere of the deck to loose her terror.

"Yes," she said, finding her voice. "I didn't know who you were."

"I thought I saw you come up here," the former star said as she joined her. Gale now saw she was wearing a smart little rain hat and long matching coat of the same material, the veil she'd been so sure she'd seen must have been conjured up by her imagination.

"I thought it would be a change," she said. The foghorn blasted and she waited to add with a smile. "It's noisy, though."

Kate nodded. "Dreadful! And I have something to tell you! Something that won't wait."

"We can go down to my cabin," Gale suggested at once. She was concerned by the troubled look on Kate Paxton's face.

The former star shook her head. "No. You come to mine." She glanced at her wristwatch. "Wait for a half-hour. I have someone to see first. I think you'll be surprised at what I have to tell you."

The foghorn blasted again. When it ended, Gale said, "Whatever you like. I'll see you in a half-hour then."

Kate only remained a minute or so longer and then made off in the fog. As soon as she left Gale decided to go on back to A Deck herself. She hadn't wanted to accompany the older actress because she had the feeling Kate might think she was joining her in an effort to discover who she was keeping the rendezvous with. It was a touchy situation.

Gale went straight to her own cabin and spent the half-hour waiting there. She had been shaken by the scare she'd received on the upper deck and had no desire to remain out in the fog alone any longer. She was also excited and puzzled by what Kate had said. Had the star found some new devastating evidence to tie Steve Benson in with the mystery? Or had she discovered something about that other suspect, the one she hadn't named.

Forty minutes passed and then Gale left her cabin to make the short journey down the dark corridor to Kate's room. When she reached it she knocked on the door. There was no answer. Again she knocked and waited. Still no answer. Perhaps she had not returned from meeting whoever it was. Before leaving Gale decided to try the door handle. To her surprise it turned easily and she was able to open the door.

When she did her eyes opened wide with horror and she gave an alarmed cry. Kate Paxton's body was suspended from the central light fixture by a scarf or some such improvised rope and swaying gently back and forth with the motion of the old vessel!

Chapter Eleven

The first person to put in an appearance in answer to Gale's frantic screams was none other than the sour little make-up man, Francois Mailet. He came quickly down the dark corridor and joined her in the doorway. When he saw the tragic sight that had so shocked her he muttered an imprecation in French and roughly seized her by the arm.

"You will come with me," he said leading her into the corridor and in the direction of the lounge. She was too close to fainting to make any protest or care. One look at the distorted features of Kate Paxton as she hung suspended there had been enough to shock and sicken her.

The make-up man saw her safely to a chair in the lounge. "Stay here. I will be back," he promised. She listened to him in a dazed fashion like a small child and sat there long after he had vanished back down the corridor.

After what seemed an eternity she was conscious of someone else coming up to her. It was Jack Henderson. At the sight of him she temporarily came out of the shock she was suffering.

"Kate! In her cabin! It's awful!" she told him in an anguished tone as she leaned forward in her chair.

Jack showed surprise. "What are you talking about?"

"Kate is dead! Go see for yourself!"

He frowned. "I don't believe it!" And he turned and ran down the corridor in the direction of the former star's cabin.

She had no clear recollection of what happened next. She knew the nurse came and talked to her soothingly. They gave her a sedative and the nurse saw her safely to bed. When she awoke the following morning she was largely herself again. The hysteria had passed but the fear and pain Kate's death had brought her was still acute. The fog still clung to the old liner and there seemed no hope of it lifting soon.

The maid brought her tea and she had breakfast in her room. She urgently wanted to discuss Kate's death with someone she could trust and so when Jack arrived at her cabin shortly before ten that morning she was relieved.

He kissed her and studied her carefully. "You're looking better," he said. "Are you sure you're well enough to talk?"

"Of course."

He sighed. "It's a nuisance not having a doctor on board. The nurse does what she can but she's no proper substitute."

Gale smiled wryly. "I don't think either the Captain or Mervin Hawley expected it to be such an eventful voyage." She sat down in one of the living-room's easy chairs. "Did I make an awful fool of myself last night?"

"No," he said at once. "They can't accuse you of that. But you were in shock and you did cry and babble a lot of things that really didn't make much sense."

"I knew what I was doing," she said with a resigned look his way, "but I couldn't stop. It was the strangest feeling. I had really lost control."

"That was apparent," he said soberly. "But out of what you did say several interesting facts emerged. For one thing you talked of meeting Kate on the upper deck and her asking you to see her in her cabin in thirty minutes."

She nodded. "Those are facts."

"The Captain gathered that," Jack said. "And he believes you must have been almost the last person who talked to Kate. He wanted me to question you about it if you were well enough to talk."

"I'm well enough," she said. "And I wasn't the last person to talk with her. I believe I was the next to the last."

He considered this with obvious surprise. "You seem very sure," he said. "On what do you base this opinion?"

"She told me she was on her way to see someone else."

"But she didn't mention who?"

"No."

Jack considered this as he took a package of cigarettes from his pocket, selected one and lit it. When he'd taken a puff he said, "And I suppose you have an idea whoever it was she met murdered her?"

Gale nodded solemnly. "That's about it."

He removed the cigarette from his lips to give her a sceptical look. "It's what I expected you'd say. It seems to me you're skipping a very plain fact. The fact that Kate Paxton took her own life."

She frowned. "I don't believe that."

"Everyone else does including the Captain and he is the legal authority on board this ship."

"But how can they think such a stupid thing?"

"It was a plain enough case," Jack said.

"She used her own scarf. The chair on which she stood to tie the scarf securely to the light fixture was exactly where she'd kicked it away from beneath her."

"Was there a suicide note?"

"No."

"I knew there couldn't be," Gale said triumphantly. "For the simple reason she didn't do it herself. When I talked to her she had no thought of taking her own life!"

Jack didn't look convinced. "I don't know how you hope to prove that," he said. "Or how you plan to show she was murdered."

"Give me time," Gale said, rising. "The Captain must have some doubts or he wouldn't have asked you to talk to me."

"Naturally there are some questions still to be answered," he admitted. "But in the main the suicide theory is accepted. I know one of the things Captain Redmore wanted to find out was whether Kate has ever mentioned suicide to you?"

"No."

He studied her carefully. "Was she in a depressed state?"

"Not especially."

"But she did seem tense, worried?"

Gale nodded. "Yes."

"Now we're getting somewhere," Jack

said with satisfaction. "Go ahead and give me the gist of your conversation."

Gale did. She was careful to leave out no details. And she finished by saying, "I'm sure she was about to tell me something really important. I think she had found out who my aunt's killer was and who we should blame for the attacks we've suffered."

Jack threw the butt of his cigarette in the fireplace and crushed it with his shoe toe.

"That was when she asked you to meet her in her cabin?"

"Yes."

"But by the time you got there she was dead.

"Pretty frustrating," he admitted.

"It's a lot more than that," she said quietly. "Up until now I have been able to blame everything on a combination of an insane Joseph Holland and the shrewdly evil Steve Benson."

"This has changed your mind?"

"Yes. Kate was very explicit. She planned to meet someone and she assured me I would be surprised by her news."

"It doesn't sound like a woman who was momentarily planning to take her own life, talking," Jack was forced to agree.

"Of course not."

He stood facing her with his hands behind his back. "But that is what we must assume she did. By all the evidence we've collected thus far she killed herself. That is how it will go down in the ship's log."

"And you'll be protecting the real murderer and giving him a chance to strike again!" she told him with bitterness.

He listened to her with friendly interest but she knew she wasn't convincing him. He just didn't believe her suspicions. He said, "I know finding poor Kate that way was a terrible shock to you. But you mustn't allow it to drive you to wild fancies."

"Very well," she said with a sigh. "What possible reason did she have for suicide?"

"According to Hawley she was very hard up. She'd been getting very little work lately."

"That may be. But she wasn't a coward. I'm sure she wasn't afraid of facing the future. She was a good actress. And she had many friends in the business. There would always have been some work."

"In a blue mood she might not have felt so sure about that," he said.

"It's not reason enough."

"It could be the gloomy atmosphere of this ship proved too much for her," Jack suggested. "I think all of us are ready to do something desperate."

"She wouldn't have asked me to come to her cabin if she had intended suicide," Gale said surprised by her own firmness, but determined to defend her friend. "She was killed by someone who was afraid she would expose him. Just as Maggie Dever was killed for the same reason."

Jack raised his eyebrows. "Then for the official verdicts of accident and suicide you want to substitute two charges of murder. Who do you think guilty? Steve Benson?"

"Maybe," she said, her eyes staring off in the distance thoughtfully. "I'm not as sure he's the murderer as I was. It could be someone else. Someone else who was on this ship that night thirty years ago when Hedda Grant vanished. A person we may have overlooked."

"I don't think I should tell the Captain that," Jack decided with a frown. "I'll just say you're surprised that Kate killed herself in the face of her conversation with you. And I'll tell him further that in view of this you think he should carefully review all the details concerning her death."

"If that's the extent to which you're prepared to back me up," she said with a rueful note of resignation in her voice.

He showed concern. "I want to believe you," he insisted. "But if I take too strong a stand it'll only work the wrong way. He'll be sure we're making too much of things and not bother looking into the matter at all."

She saw that he had a point. "Very well," she said. "You handle it as you think best."

He left her and she remained in the cabin alone for awhile. She heard the engines far below take on a more lively vibration and decided the fog must have lifted a little and Captain Redmore had given instructions to increase the old ship's speed. Weary of being in the cabin she put on her trenchcoat and waterproof kerchief and went out on the deck. Contrary to her expectations the fog had not lifted. It was still as bad as before.

She had no intentions of going to the upper deck. It would only remind her of Kate and she hadn't fully accepted the former star's death even yet. Kate Paxton had been one of the few on the *Britannia* whom she felt to be her friend. Now she was gone. The memory of that gently swaying body, the feet a good distance above the carpeted floor and the distorted, purple face that had once known beauty still haunted her. She gave a small shiver as she walked along the deck.

Everything was sopping wet from the heavy mist. The foghorn above continued to blast its warning signal and the doomed liner was shrouded in the sinister grey mist so that everything took on a wraith-like and eerie look. It was dark even at this early hour of the day. There would be no work on the picture while the weather remained like this and they could not even head back to port.

Thinking of the picture brought her thoughts to a different track. Kate Paxton had played an important role in the original ending. Hawley had intended to film an entirely different ending making Steve Benson the villain, but would he be able to do it now that Kate was dead? Not unless Jack wrote her out of the scene and this might leave an awkward loose end. A character who dropped out of the story without explanation. It would present a problem. She wished she had asked Jack about it when he'd visited her cabin earlier.

She was well in the forward section of the big liner now, in the area where they had filmed many of the important exterior scenes. Suddenly she came upon a familiar figure in an unusual spot. The diminutive Francois Mailet was leaning against the railing near the bow and staring moodily down at the fog-shrouded water far below. He was hatless and his grey hair rustled slightly in the gentle breeze. He was so preoccupied with his own thoughts he seemed unaware that she had come up beside him. She felt she should speak since it was their first meeting since that moment of horror when he had come to her rescue in the doorway of Kate's cabin.

"Hello," she said. "I wanted to thank you for yesterday."

The little man turned to her slowly, a look of surprise on his pinched face and the eyes behind the thick glasses holding a strange look. He seemed to be having difficulty remembering although she couldn't imagine why he should.

Finally he said, "Oh, yes, yesterday," in his odd voice. "Well, it was lucky I happened to be passing."

"I don't know what would have happened to me otherwise."

The little man scowled. "You'd have survived."

"Perhaps. But I was in an awful state."

"It wasn't a pleasant business," Francois Mailet said. "But then this whole voyage has been a mistake. Hawley has made us all pay the price for his folly."

"You honestly feel that way?"

"Yes. And I'm not the only one."

"I know that," she said. "Well, it's about over now anyway."

"Not until we reach New York again," the little man said testily. "And if we continue to be fogbound like this that may be quite awhile."

She sighed. "Do you think we'll be doing any more work on the picture now that Kate is gone?"

The make-up man shrugged. "You can't tell about Hawley. I hear he has some big idea. You can be certain whatever it is it'll spell trouble for the rest of us."

Gale could tell she was beginning to annoy the peculiar little man so she said goodbye and turned and made her way back along the deck again. She wondered what Hawley's idea might be and when he would broach it to them all. It wasn't long before she found out. At lunch there was a notice for a company call in the forward lounge at two that afternoon.

She was there a few minutes before two and took a seat where she wouldn't be too conspicuous not far from Steve Benson and Jane Fair. She felt strangely out of place and lonely without the friendly Kate at her elbow to whisper some sharp comment or point out some important face. Jack Henderson, who had not shown up at lunch, now entered in the company of Mervin Hawley and she decided that he and the famous director had probably been working on the script through the lunch hour.

She was proven correct in her assumption when Mervin Hawley took the centre of the lounge to address the company. In part, he told them, "We have only a few days more to complete our picture. The *Britannia* is due back in New York on Saturday. I've learned there is every chance the weather will remain bad until then. It probably won't clear up until we're ready to head for port. So this will make it impossible to do any more exteriors."

He paused a moment and there were a few comments from the various actors and technicians gathered in the big lounge. Gale thought Steve Benson looked pleased. Again she wondered about the guilt of the handsome leading man.

Her attention was taken as Mervin Hawley resumed his address to the gathered company. "You all know," he said, "that I am not satisfied with the present ending of the film."

Gale glanced automatically in Steve

Benson's direction and saw his handsome face take on an angry flush. He leaned forward and whispered something in Jane Fair's ear and she nodded her agreement. Then they both stared at Hawley with resentful eyes.

The big man went on, "The suicide of our dear Kate Paxton has added to our problems. I know she was loved by you all. Speaking for myself I can only say I have lost one of my closest friends. Not only a friend but a valued co-worker. Up until late last night I felt it would be impossible to film the proposed new ending without her. That we would have to be satisfied with the picture as it now stands." He paused dramatically. "Happily we have hit on a solution."

Mervin Hawley now leaned over and took a script from Jack and held it up for them all to see. "Thanks to the ingenuity of our author we have a new ending. And one we can shoot regardless of the weather since it takes place inside. Also it is an ending in which we will be able to cover up the absence of Kate since the scene will deal with a masked ball. A masked ball held on board ship to mark the final night of the voyage."

He paused for the murmurs of approval

that came from all sides. Gale saw that Steve Benson was not one of those who had joined in. He was sitting with a frown marring the classic profile.

"I may say there was no ball on that night thirty years ago when the real Hedda vanished. But there was a party, a gay one, and I danced with Hedda several times. So the idea of a masked ball is actually in accord with what really happened. We will use an actress resembling Kate in size and colouring to act her role and she will remain masked throughout the scene to cover the substitution. Because we are having an unusually calm sea I have planned to film the scene in the ballroom tonight. The wardrobe mistress will have your masks ready."

With that the meeting came to an end. The gathered crowd broke up into small groups with special interests to discuss. Gale saw Steve Benson and Jane Fair go quickly to the nearest exit and leave without waiting to pick up the new scene or to bother speaking to Mervin Hawley. Jack had seen her and now he was coming across the room with her copy of the scene in his hand.

"Well, what do you say to that?" he asked as he gave it to her.

"It sounds all right," she said. "I don't think Steve is happy."

"Anything but. But his contract leaves him no choice. He'll have to play the part whatever way I write it."

"I take it he's still the villain."

"In the scene, yes," Jack said. "I haven't decided about him in real life."

"Did you have a talk with the Captain?"

"I managed a few words in the short time Hawley gave me to myself."

She said, "Did he promise to look more carefully into Kate's supposed suicide?"

"He promised that he would," Jack said. "I think he's more worried about this fog situation and getting the *Britannia* back to New York."

"No doubt," she said bitterly.

They were still talking when the director came over to join them. Hawley smiled at her. "You're looking fine again," he said.

"I'm not feeling all that well."

"Don't fret," he assured her. "We'll soon have the picture wrapped up and you'll be safely back in New York. You have some good extra lines in this new scene." He smiled for Jack's benefit. "Trust your writer friend to look after that. And when this picture is released it's my belief you'll be made as a star."

She managed a faint smile. "So much has been happening I'd forgotten about this being my first starring role."

"We've been putting together some of the first part of the story," Hawley told her. "And you can take my word for it you're great! There are times when I wonder if it's not Hedda herself up there on the screen."

She stared at him. His face had taken on an animated expression and there was a strange brightness in his eyes that almost frightened her. She remembered all the things Kate Paxton had told her about him. Kate had known so much about those far-off days. She had said that Hawley had once been madly in love with Hedda but she had treated him as she had all the others. She could not see this strong-willed man taking easily to the role of the discarded lover. Yet Hedda must have had some strong hold on him until the very end for it was clear that he was still obsessed by her memory.

"I'm glad you're satisfied," she said quietly.

"I'm more than satisfied, I'm delighted," he told her. "A lot of people criticised me for picking an unknown for Hedda's role. The talk was I was more interested in cashing in on publicity than in developing talent. But we'll show them they were wrong. You are making Hedda live again!"

She nodded but her thoughts were wandering. Who was it had told her of Kate's love affair with Jerry Hall? She couldn't clearly remember now. She thought it had been Hawley himself. That meant that Kate and Hedda must have been enemies since unfaithful as Hedda had been she'd continued to show jealousy where her husband was concerned. What a tangled skein it had been! Not much wonder it had ended in Hedda's violent death and this strange sequel on the same ship a full three decades later.

She excused herself from the company of Jack and the director and went back to her own cabin to study the new ending. She did have some extra lines and good ones. She thought the scene was clever and with her exit the camera would suggest that she had gone to her death. Later there would be a showdown scene on the dance floor and Steve Benson would confess to pushing her over the side of the great liner. She settled down to learning her lines.

When she sat beside Steve at dinner that evening he appeared morose and not eager for conversation. However she made it a point to ask him, "How do you feel about the new ending?"

"It's even worse than the other one," he complained.

"But Mr. Hawley feels it will improve the picture," she said.

"It will never be shown," he promised. "As soon as we get back to New York I'm calling in my lawyers. I'll stop Hawley from using the new version."

She saw that it was pointless to discuss this with the unhappy actor so she quickly changed the subject. "Have they found any trace of the escaped lunatic?" she asked.

"Holland?" He shook his head. "No. And they're not likely to."

"But they did find his coat and hat somewhere below?"

"He may have been on board for awhile," Steve Benson acknowledged. "But I think he's gone over the side long before this. He always had suicidal tendencies you know."

"I had heard he was moody," she agreed.

"We'll all be lunatics," the actor said grumpily, "if we have to stay cooped up on this ship much longer."

Gale gave up trying to talk to him and devoted the rest of her time at the table between Mervin Hawley and the Captain.

Dinner over she went directly to the dressing room and put on the elaborate blue gown which she would be using for the scene. The wardrobe mistress gave her a wide silver mask and then she went in for Francois Mailet to do her make-up. The little man was in a tense state and barking a string of orders to his nervous girl assistant. She hardly said a word to him as he worked on her with his usual patience. And she felt a surge of relief when she left him to go on the set.

It was the beginning of a long and trying evening. The scene was a complicated one with orchestra cues and a group of extras to be worked in as guests at the ball. Steve gave a wooden, poor performance and he and Hawley had several rows during the filming.

The ballroom was crowded and noisy. There were the several heavy sound cameras and other equipment. And the giant floodlights blazed on cruelly giving off a sickening heat. Several times Gale felt as if the mask was suffocating her. And when she had a break between her scenes she decided to step out on the deck briefly for some fresh air.

She was afraid if she asked for permission Hawley might refuse it so she waited until he and Jack were busy discussing the next take and hurried out a handy exit onto the damp deck. Almost at once the feeling of being stifled left her.

It was still as foggy and eerie as before and the arrival of darkness made it impossible to see any distance at all. Yet she was glad to be outside and away from the tension of the set for a few minutes. She gave a deep sigh as she stood by the railing.

Then from behind her she heard a shuffling movement and a hoarse male voice said, "Hedda! Hedda as lovely as ever!"

She wheeled around in surprise and fear to find herself staring at a small, bent man with an ugly, twisted face, a face covered with a thick stubble of white beard. He was completely bald but the thing that terrified her above all else was the strange gleam in his eyes. He had the too bright eyes of a madman. And now he came slowly toward her, the claw-like hands reaching out!

Chapter Twelve

"Hedda!" the caricature of a man pleaded. "Don't you know me? It's Joe!"

She pressed back against the railing and cried out. But the same moment the fog-horn above gave a loud blast and the scream for help was drowned by it. Slowly the weird creature edged closer to her and the filthy claws were now caressing her dress.

"I've been waiting to talk to you Hedda!" the madman said eagerly.

She screamed again and tried to dodge to one side but the hands caught her and held her in an insane grip. Now she struggled and tried to push him away conscious of the odour of his clothes and his fetid, hot breath as he pressed his face close to hers and gabbled in her ear.

"Gale!" It was Jack's welcome voice that rang out across the deck. At the sound of it the madman quickly released her and glanced in the direction from which the shout had come. Seeing Jack running forward with Mervin Hawley at his side the

253

bald man turned and ran off into the fog with his peculiar shuffling gait.

She was clutching the rail for support and sobbing when Jack came up to her. "All right?" he asked.

"Yes," she managed. "It's Holland!"

"I know," he said and ran on in the direction in which the little man had disappeared. Mervin Hawley had already gone on after him.

Gale was trembling and chilled with fear and having been out in the cold dampness for longer than she'd planned. But she remained where she was to see what happened. And a few minutes later the two men came back with the struggling madman between them as their prisoner.

When they came up to her the bald, dishevelled Joseph Holland glared at her. "You're not Hedda!" he snarled. "You're a fake! It's all a fake!"

Jack said, "We'll turn him over to the Captain. I'll see you inside." And they moved on to the entrance of the corridor.

The excitement attending the capture of Joseph Holland was on a level with the shock that had been felt by everyone on the fogbound *Britannia* when Kate Paxton's suicide had been discovered. It meant there would be no more work and

Mervin Hawley dismissed the company and issued a call for the completion of the new ending the following morning at ten.

About an hour after the quite mad Joseph Holland had been safely locked up in the ship's brig Gale found herself in the Captain's office again with Mervin Hawley and Jack. The Captain showed himself to be in a much better frame of mind now that the worry of the stowaway had been finally settled.

Standing by his desk, Captain Redmore said, "Finding Joseph Holland goes a long way to solving several of the riddles that have been puzzling us."

Hawley nodded. "True! He is certainly the one who attacked Jack and then went after Gale in the pool."

Captain Redmore agreed, saying, "I don't think there is any question of that. We can also chalk up some of the other mysterious events to him."

Gale, who was sitting across from the desk, spoke up, "Do you think he had anything to do with Kate Paxton's death?"

The Captain frowned. "Miss Paxton took her own life."

"Are you so sure?" Gale questioned.

Mervin Hawley looked at her. "You must get the idea she was murdered out of your mind," he advised. "It doesn't make sense. What motive would Holland have?"

"He's all mixed up about the past and present. Kate played a part in his past. He could have hated her for some reason not known to any of us and taken his revenge by throttling her and making it seem a suicide."

"Fantastic!" Hawley jeered. Jack gave her an appealing look not to continue discussing the matter along these lines, but she was firm in her stand, feeling she owed this much loyalty to the dead Kate.

The Captain looked faintly upset. "My dear Miss Bond," he said, "all the evidence in the tragic incident indicated it was suicide. The overturned chair, the lack of any sort of struggle, the way the knot was tied! I feel the matter is settled."

"I see," she said quietly.

"I have contacted New York," the Captain went on, "and advised the authorities there we now have Joseph Holland in custody. I think everyone is relieved."

Mervin Hawley nodded. "There's no telling what crime he might have committed if we hadn't caught up with him. He was certainly about to do Miss Bond harm when we surprised him."

The interview ended on that self-satisfied note. There seemed a general agreement that with the capture of the insane artist all problems on board the old liner had been solved. Mervin Hawley even went so far as to suggest Holland must have been the one who had pushed Hedda Grant overboard on that fateful night thirty years earlier and had been about to repeat his crime when they'd interrupted him. Neither Jack nor the Captain appeared taken with this easy solution to the ancient mystery although they made no arguments.

Jack escorted her back to her cabin and stayed a moment to talk. She threw herself in an easy chair and frowned up at him. "So this is how it's going to end," she said. "With everyone congratulating everyone else on their brilliance and blaming this madman for all that has happened."

The young writer stood before her with an amused expression on his boyish face. "I would have thought you'd be especially pleased. We now have an explanation for almost everything."

"Almost everything," she reminded him. "It isn't good enough for me."

"You should be thankful to know you're in no more danger."

She said, "If that is the true picture."

"But of course it is," he said with a trace of impatience. "I am willing to go along with your thinking as long as there were legitimate doubts. I'd say Holland's capture ends them. So why go on trying to build a mystery where none really exists?"

She smiled bitterly. "You want an easy happy ending too!"

He nodded. "Is that such a crime? Especially when I want it badly because it means you'll be safe."

There was such a genuine sincerity in his manner she was momentarily touched. Jack must have been under a dreadful strain worrying about her all these weeks. It was natural that he would be delighted now that the shadow threatening her had seemingly been removed.

She held out a hand. "I'm sorry, darling," she said. "I suppose I am being very feminine and difficult."

He moved a step closer and took her hand in both of his and caressed it. "I don't blame you for feeling as you do. You've been through a lot. But you must be careful not to let it make you a permanent neurotic."

Gale laughed. "That sounds very serious."

"It could be."

"Perhaps it is this old ship," she observed with a sigh. "The yesterday atmosphere so filled with the mystery of my aunt's vanishing and the gloomy fog that has kept us out here virtually prisoners. Maybe when we get back to New York I'll feel differently."

He still held her hand. "I hope so."

"Mervin Hawley is determined to continue filming his new ending it seems," she said.

"He'll be able to wind it up in the morning. If the weather clears we should be heading back to port at once."

"Will you be flying back to Hollywood right away?"

"Will you?" he asked.

"I think so," she said with a faint smile. "I'm a little homesick."

"Come to think of it so am I," he admitted with a smile of his own. "Maybe we can use the plane trip back to get some things settled."

She showed surprise. "What sort of things?"

"What our plans are going to be for the future," he said with meaning in his voice and in his expression.

Gale preferred to tease him. She said lightly, "That's something you'll have to

259

take up with my agent."

"No agent better try to interfere with the plans I have in mind," he warned her. And he drew her up to him and took her in his arms for a lasting kiss. It was a good moment. A moment of mutual understanding and faith in the future. And when she finally said goodnight to the red-haired young writer and began her preparations for bed she was as happy as she had been since coming on board the *Britannia*.

Tomorrow would wind up the film. And within a day or two they should be back in New York and away from the *Britannia* with all her reminders of the tragic past. These were the thoughts going through her mind as she crossed to turn off the light in the living-room.

Just as she reached for the switch there was a knock on her cabin door and a moment later an envelope was slipped under it. She stared at the envelope in some surprise and then went over and picked it up. She opened the door and glanced out in the corridor but whoever had delivered the message had vanished. Closing the door and bolting it she now gave her attention to the envelope.

Opening it she found a single sheet inside on which had been hastily scrawled

"Meet me on the forward section of A Deck at once. Something urgent to tell you!" It was signed with the initials S.B.

Gale frowned as she read the note a second time. The initials indicated it must have come from Steve Benson. Could this be the moment she'd been waiting for? The turning point when Steve would reveal the truth about himself? Her first thought was to phone Jack in his cabin. But then she hesitated. It might be too soon for that. If she brought anyone else into this she would surely frighten the leading man and likely he would reveal nothing. He had asked her to go out and meet him alone and that is what she must do. Surely he wouldn't attempt to harm her even if he was deeply involved in what had happened in the past. It would do him no good and expose him to fresh danger of being apprehended.

Convincing herself of this she quickly dressed again and put on her trenchcoat and kerchief and hurried out of the cabin to keep her rendezvous with the troubled Steve. It could be he was merely still indignant about being forced to become the villain of the film and was about to enlist her aid in a stand against producer Hawley.

As soon as she stepped out on deck Gale

261

saw the fog still as thick as ever. She had become so accustomed to the old liner's foghorn bleating its warning she barely heard it when she was in her cabin. But now in the grey loneliness of the glistening wet deck it was an ominous sound. She walked the deserted length from her cabin to the bow conscious of the slight heaving of the ship and stalked by the shrouded sentinels of such familiar things as companionways, lifeboats creaking eerily and deck chairs that seemed to have ghostly occupants that turned out to be merely rumpled blankets as you came closer to them.

It was a haunted atmosphere!

Only her desire to see Steve and hear what he had to say had made her brave this lonely walk. She could only see a few feet ahead and she knew that he would not be able to see her approach until she was right upon him. This seemed an advantage. And the heavy mist would also provide a curtain to hide them from anyone else as they had this after-midnight chat.

Now she was far forward in the open section of the bow at its broadest point. She peered through the mist in an effort to see some sign of Steve but he was nowhere in sight. Had it been a stupid joke played on her by someone? Or had he merely grown tired of waiting and left? Dismay swept through her as she stood there with a perplexed expression on her pretty face. She could hear the swishing of the waves as the *Britannia* ploughed slowly ahead, the groaning of the old liner's weary plates, the steady thump of the engines far below.

She waited for several minutes. Then she crossed to the weather side of the ship. She would have expected Steve to be waiting on the other side but it was hard to tell. She clutched the railing and made up her mind she would stay there only a few minutes longer and then return to her cabin. Her heart was beating at too fast a pace and she was on the verge of trembling. She was frightened of being alone out there at this late hour.

And then almost as if a cold, clammy hand had reached out to nudge her she knew she was no longer alone. She turned and saw the figure coming slowly out of the mist toward her. But it wasn't Steve! It was the phantom creature! The ghost of the long missing Hedda Grant!

Gale raised her clenched fist to her mouth to break her cry of horror. She was frozen to the spot where she stood. And the spectre came closer each minute.

All the details were right. The woman wore a pillbox hat, and there was a veil, no mistaking that this time, and the fashionable clothes of another era that so weirdly set the apparition apart. The wraith-like figure was within a few feet of her now and although Gale could not make her out clearly at least she was aware of two things. The spectre had a certain solidity and she held a small gun in her right hand.

And now she spoke in a low voice, "I was afraid you mightn't come."

Gale spoke in an awed whisper, "Who are you?"

"Surely you recognise me," there was derision in the low voice. "I'm your aunt, Hedda Grant."

"No!" Gale said drawing back. "I don't believe you."

"You should know me well enough since you've been playing me in this film. And badly I may say!"

The foghorn above blasted drowning out anything that might be said. Gale pressed tightly against the railing and debated whether she dared try to race for freedom. But that ugly little gun was pointed at her dangerously near and she knew her chances of escaping alive would be small.

Again she said, "Who are you? What do you want?"

The figure in the veil chuckled harshly. "Let us say I have a small account to settle with you!"

"What are you talking about?"

"You've tried to destroy my memory! Usurp my name! You must have known I would never let you do that!"

Gale stared at the weird figure in the mist certain that she recognised the voice and not able to remember where. She said, "You're mad! Hedda Grant has been dead thirty years! Why pretend to be her?"

"Because I am Hedda Grant!"

Gale was certain now she was dealing with some insane person. Swallowing hard she said, "Then you must know I meant you no harm! I'm your niece!"

"I know all about that!" the phantom of the fog gloated. "You are her daughter! And you lack real ability just as she did!"

"You mustn't say such things about my mother!" Gale protested.

"Though I must say you do have more spirit. It's too bad you have to die," the wraith went on, "but you must join Maggie and Kate Paxton!"

She gasped. "Then they were murdered! And you're the one!"

265

"No harm in your knowing now," the figure said. "Maggie talked too much and in the end she refused to help me murder you. I do not tolerate disloyal people so I staged her accident."

"Poor Maggie!"

"You may well mourn her. She was your friend. And so was Kate. But that was to be expected! Kate always took sides against me! She even stole my husband from me. Not that it did her much good."

A strange coldness crept through Gale. She stared at the eerie figure and in a dazed tone said, "You know everything! You talk as if you really were Hedda Grant returned from the ocean!"

"I am Hedda Grant, back from my watery grave," the figure said mockingly. "A restful hiding place. But then you'll know all about that soon. For that is where you are going."

"No!" she edged along the rail a little.

The phantom followed her. "Don't try to get away. I'm an excellent shot," the voice said sharply. "We can't have another accident or even a suicide so we'll just have you vanish over the rail. That will make an excellent finish to this miserable attempt to steal my glory."

"What are you saying?"

"I'm saying that your death will be written down as the second mysterious vanishing from the *Britannia*. They are bound to link it with what happened to me. So in a way you'll share my fame whether I like it or not. But I can be generous. I'm willing to be fair. Because a second vanishing is going to make the legend more widely known than ever. We'll be talked about whenever mysteries of the sea are discussed for all time!"

"You are mad," Gale insisted. "To talk this way and imagine you're Hedda!"

"Must I tell you again," the woman in the veil said sharply. "I am Hedda."

And it was then that Gale became certain about the voice. At last she knew where she had heard it before and the revelation left her faint with awe and fear. She stared at the figure holding the gun.

"No!" she said. "You can't be!"

"So you've finally guessed," the veiled woman said. "Well, I expected that you would."

"You've been among us all along," Gale gasped. "Planning your murders! Working your evil!"

For an answer the woman with the gun used her free hand to lift up her veil and revealed her face. It was the pinched, wan face Gale had known as belonging to Francois Mailet!

"Are you satisfied?" the high-pitched familiar voice snapped.

"I don't understand!" Gale said, bewildered.

"Really very simple," the figure with the gun said. "I am Hedda Grant. For years I've been posing as Francois Mailet. You wouldn't know but for a long time I did a male impersonation in a vaudeville act. When my world collapsed I went back to the Chicago area and began doing the act again in night clubs under a different name. After Jerry was killed I began drinking more than ever. I gave up even the work in the clubs. I spent some time in a sanatorium. When I came out I decided to call myself Francois Mailet, pretend I was a man and establish myself as a beautician. I did so well I finally was able to go back to Hollywood and get movie work. No one recognised me. The few that were still alive wouldn't expect to see me out there, certainly not as a male, and I had lost my looks to the extent I didn't have to worry anyway." Hedda's voice was bitter.

"But why? And why did you pretend to vanish? To be drowned?"

The pinched face showed scorn. "Maggie

gave you the clue to that but you were too stupid to recognise it. My husband, Jerry, had been having an affair with my personal maid. I knew about it and couldn't stop them since my own record for faithfulness was nothing to brag about. I'd been drinking too much. The girl and I had a quarrel. I stabbed her. I killed her. She was the first person I ever killed. Jerry came to the cabin and found me on my knees by the body. He had loved the girl and he cursed me for what I had done. I begged him to help me. And he offered to at last for a price. It was a big price. I had to die!"

"To die?" In spite of her terror Gale was fascinated.

"He was clever and he thought it all out quickly. I was to assume the identity of the maid. Using her glasses and clothes and dying my hair to match hers would make it possible to pass myself off as her. In the meantime Jerry waited for a quiet time in the night and went out and tossed the body of the girl he had loved into the ocean. He promised to shield me from the authorities as suffering shock from the death of my mistress and get me safely ashore. He also insisted that I go to the midwest and live the life of a nonentity. It was his revenge for what I'd done. He knew I prized my fame above all else."

"And you agreed to it?"

"It was that or face a murder charge," Hedda Grant said. "Jerry didn't care since my career was in bad shape and we owed a lot more money than I could hope to earn. So he abandoned me. Left me alone in a cheap Chicago hotel to read my own death notices. He didn't gain much. Within a year he was killed in that plane crash."

"Couldn't you have revealed yourself then?"

Hedda Grant shook her head. "It was too late. There would be too many things to explain. I was drinking a lot and didn't care any longer. I had one glorious memory. My disappearance had been made a front page affair. I had enjoyed the headlines again. And I knew the story would live on through the years as it has."

Gale said, "But don't you see how wrong you've been?"

"I've protected my fame," the figure with the gun said arrogantly. "I'm entitled to that. When I heard about Hawley's plan to make the picture and hire you to play my role I knew what I had to do. And now the time has come to do it!"

"No!" Gale screamed. And she edged

forward and ran toward the extreme point of the bow.

Hedda Grant kept her word. She fired at her and Gale felt a sharp stinging in her left arm where the bullet must have struck her and then the warmth of the blood that spurted from the wound. Near fainting she pushed on as far as she could go. Hedda fired again and missed.

And now there were shouts and the clatter of footsteps as members of the crew on the night watch came forward to inquire into the shots. Hedda Grant had betrayed herself. The frail figure in the weird clothes of another generation came running up to the point of the bow where Gale had retreated.

"You little vixen!" she cried. And she fired again. But again she missed. And now her pursuers were upon her. With a wild angry glance in Gale's direction she moved to the rail, raised herself and with a wailing scream dropped down into the mist-shrouded sea.

One of the sailors came forward and took Gale in his arms for support while the other left to sound the alarm to lower a life-boat and look for the missing woman. Gale collapsed at that point and so she knew nothing of the exhaustive search that was made.

It was no surprise that under the conditions the body was not found.

Gale's injured arm brought a halt to the filming. There was no question of the second ending being completed which was entirely to the worried Steve Benson's satisfaction. And although the weather cleared the next morning and the *Britannia* was able to turn around and head for New York there was no activity on the part of the film company.

Gale woke to find herself in her cabin with the nurse looking after her. Her first request was to talk to Jack and he was not slow in arriving. As soon as they were alone, she asked him, "What do they know about it?"

"Not much," he said. "Except that Francois Mailet went off his head and dressed as a woman tried to shoot you. When he didn't succeed and knew he was going to be captured he jumped overboard."

"So they didn't find him?"

Jack shook his head. "No. Whatever made you go out to meet him like that? You had been warned. You knew the danger! And why would he want to harm you?"

Then she told him. He listened with

growing incredulity. She finished by saying, "Since they don't know I wonder if they should be told?"

Jack frowned. "You want to conceal her crimes?"

"Will anything be gained by revealing them?" she asked.

He hesitated. "I'll discuss it with the Captain."

Early in the afternoon the Captain and Jack came to her room together. Captain Redmore inquired about her arm and seemed glad to know that she had suffered only a minor flesh wound. He continued to discuss the night's events standing rather awkwardly at the foot of her bed.

Jack sat down beside the bed and with a knowing glance her way said, "I've told the Captain your story."

Captain Redmore cleared his throat. "I've considered it very carefully, Miss Bond, and I'm inclined to think you're right. The official log of the *Britannia* will show that shortly after midnight last night one, Francois Mailet, became demented and after attacking you and at the point of capture chose to throw himself into the sea."

"Thank you," she said quietly. Knowing that now the nightmare, like the fog that had accompanied it, was truly over. The pendulum of fate had swung full around to make Hedda Grant's drowning of thirty years before a reality. The book could be closed. She turned to Jack with a meaning look and he nodded slowly to show his understanding and approval.